The Accidental Duke

By Sandra Schehl

Copyright © 2020 Willow and Oak Press
All rights reserved.

Dedication
This is dedicated to my husband Doug, whose love and support made this book possible.

I also want to recognize my good friends and critique partners Christine Logothetis and Leslie Thomas. Without them, these words would still be hidden away.

Table of Contents

Chapter One
Chapter Two
Chapter Three
Chapter Four
Chapter Five
Chapter Six
Chapter Seven
Chapter Eight
Chapter Nine
Chapter Ten
Chapter Eleven
Chapter Twelve
Chapter Thirteen
Chapter Fourteen
Chapter Fifteen
Chapter Sixteen
Chapter Seventeen
Chapter Eighteen
Chapter Nineteen
Chapter Twenty
Chapter Twenty-One

Chapter Twenty-Two
Chapter Twenty-Three
Chapter Twenty-Four
Chapter Twenty-Five
Chapter Twenty-Six
Chapter Twenty-Seven
Chapter Twenty-Eight
<u>Chapter Twenty-Nine</u>
Chapter Thirty
Chapter Thirty-One
Chapter Thirty-Two
Chapter Thirty-Three
Chapter Thirty-Four

Chapter One

Mar 15th, 1841

David frowned. The incessant pounding in his dream seemed unending. Reluctantly, he raised an eyelid, to see that sunlight was peeking through the gap in the drapes of the window. The pounding had stopped for a few moments, then resumed. "Your Grace," a feminine voice called out. "Please, open the door. I have news of the Duchess." David sat up quickly, immediately regretting the movement. He clutched his head to assure that it would not go rolling off his shoulders. Gathering his faculties, he stood up, knocking an empty bottle off the settee. He looked around for his dressing gown, only to realize that he was still in his clothes from the night before, and in the salon, not his bedroom.

Stumbling to the door of his London townhouse, he threw it open just as a small fist was poised to resume pounding again. The door's assailant stumbled forward and he caught her against him. For a moment, he basked in the feel, the scent of her. Clarissa. Even as she pulled out of his grasp and straightened he was assaulted by the scent of lemon verbena, the scent of Clarissa.

He remembered how he'd saved his coin for two whole months when he was a boy and walked to the village apothecary by himself, to buy her a bottle of the perfume, which he presented to her on their shared tenth birthday. She'd worn it from that day on. More than anything, this scent was home to him, and he breathed in deeply. She froze in his arms, then immediately took a step back, and lifted her chin as if preparing herself for battle.

"Your Grace, I've been sent here to retrieve you. Your mother is not well. She needs you to return to Hollister House right away," Clarissa told him. It took a moment for him to absorb her words. The Duchess was ill? Realizing she still stood on his doorstep, he opened his door, and drew her inside.

"Come in, so we may talk." He led her through the entry, back to the salon, where he had inadvertently spent the night. Clarissa looked around at the mess, and he wished at once he hadn't let her inside, realizing what it must look like to her eyes.

Several months ago, he had fired all of the servants, once he discovered they were all reporting his activities back to the Duchess. He had not replaced them, or seen any need to. He was perfectly capable of cleaning after himself, dressing and feeding himself. Appearances to the contrary, he reasoned. He could tell Clarissa was wisely holding her tongue, even as her eyes grew wide at the piles of papers and books and bits of clothing strewn on every surface. The Clarissa of his youth would have had no compunction about lecturing him on his lack of tidiness. This Clarissa did not see it as her place to comment. He had the urge to quickly go about, and pick it all up, but realized that would look foolish. Instead, he took her to the settee and pushed a stack of papers aside so she could sit down. She carefully sat down on the edge. Her hands knotted in her lap. He sat in an armchair across from her.

"Now, tell me, what's going on? Why have you come all the way to London?"

"She's written you several times, but you have never replied. Your man of business has reported that you refuse to speak of your mother, or hear any news of her. Your Grace, she's been sick for some time." She stopped, as if suddenly all the starch had gone out of her spine, and she looked momentarily lost. He waited patiently as she took a deep breath, and continued. "The surgeon has been to see her; she had a tumor in her breast. He excised the breast, but apparently it was discovered too late, and this disease has spread. She grows weaker. I fear she has not much time weeks, a few months perhaps. It is so like when Mama..." She stopped, her voice choked and he saw tears in her eyes, before she hastily looked away. He waited while she gathered herself.

"Please," she implored. "I know you and the Duchess have had your differences, but she is your mother. She needs you. Hollister House needs you. I am not leaving here without you." She said, once again stiffening her backbone against any objection he would have. Her words alarmed him. How long had the Duchess been ill? He looked down at the pile of unopened letters in his mother's hand, carelessly thrown on the floor. Guilt ate away at him. He stood up, and Clarissa stood up with him. Her hands clenched at her sides. He knew at once she assumed he was dismissing her. He shook his head.

"I will go with you. I must pack and clean myself up, first. We'll leave within the hour." He told her. She blinked in surprise, and then nodded in relief.

"Your Grace, if you will go bathe, I would be happy to pack your trunk, if you would show me where it is."

"Of course, thank you. Follow me."

He felt strange, leading her into his bed chamber. There was a time he would have laid down his life to have her in this room, a time she might have happily followed him here. He sighed, there was no use even letting his mind wander down that path. Not anymore. He went to his closet and pulled a valise from a shelf, and handed it to her, as well as a small trunk from the floor of the closet "Just pack an assortment of shirts and breeches. The small cloths, cravats and stockings are in the drawers to the left in that bureau." He pointed. She nodded and immediately got to work pulling shirts out, and folding them to place them in a pile on the bureau, readying them for packing.

He excused himself and went to his wash room. Not wanting to waste any time heating water, he would make due with a cold wash and shave. He pulled off his clothing and shivered as he ran the cool wet cloth over every inch of exposed skin.

He shaved as quickly as he dared; wishing he had thought to get his hair trimmed this week. His mother was always beseeching him for the state of his hair. The dark mahogany curls were unruly at the best of times and unless he kept it closely trimmed, it looked unkempt. The last time his mother had seen him she told him he looked like a pirate, and she hadn't meant it as a compliment. He sighed. There was nothing he could do about it now.

One last glance in the mirror told him his brown eyes were still bloodshot, but at least he was clean shaven and a bit less rough around the edges. He longed for some tea, or better yet, coffee, to sweep away the last of the cobwebs. He could only blame himself that there was no one to make it for him. He pulled on the dressing gown hanging on the back of the door of his washroom, and strode back to his bedroom.

Clarissa was just buckling the straps on his valise, where it lay on his bed and the trunk was closed, secured. She looked up, and her eyes grew wide, seeing him in his dressing gown. She stiffened, her face turning scarlet, and averted her eyes. He would have laughed at her reaction if it didn't make him so damned sad.

"I...I'll go tell MacPherson we'll be leaving soon," she said, grabbing the bag and heading for the bedchamber door. He stepped in front of her, and she stilled in mid-stride, and then took a half a step back. She looked anywhere, but at him.

"I'll take that," he said. She frowned, not sure what he was talking about.

"The valise, I'll take it down. I'll just be a few minutes."

She nodded and set the valise on the floor. He stepped aside she spared him a blushing glance, before scurrying out the door. Shaking his head, he went to his closet and pulled on his clothes. He dispensed with a cravat, not wanting to worry about knotting it just so. He was about to embark on two days of travel and only wanted to be comfortable. He pulled on his boots, and dragged his trunk and valise down the stairs and placed them next to the door, then went about the townhouse, making sure he had not left any lamps or fires burning, from the night before. It was then he heard a sleepy voice coming down the stairs.

"Going somewhere, Hollister?" His friend Viscount Kenton Fairchild asked, as he buttoned his shirt and ran a hand through his golden, sleep tousled locks. David had completely forgotten that he had spent the night-or morning actually, after delivering him home from their night's adventure.

"I am going home to Hollister House. My mother is very ill. It appears to be serious," he told his friend.

"I am sorry to hear that. Would you like me to come with you?" Fairchild offered. David was touched and humbled at the offer.

"No, there is no telling how long I may be. Besides, you have your own family issues to deal with, right now, if I'm not mistaken."

"Don't remind me," Fairchild scoffed. "If the Duchess is still demanding you marry, remember, you may have your pick of the Fairchild woman. You have four to choose from...no, now that is five. Now that Olivia is newly widowed. That bloody bastard, Lord Winfield, having the bad grace to die in a duel after bedding another man's wife," he said bitterly. David knew that following the death of her husband and the resulting scandal, Lady Winfield was ensconced at

Fairchild's home, along with all of his sisters and his mother; hence the reason Fairchild was staying with him.

"You may stay here as long as you like, Fairchild. In fact, I would appreciate it if you would reside here, while I am away. That would save me having to close up the place. I do not know when I shall be back. Clarissa came in the family coach, and I will be returning with her. You know where my horse is stabled. If you will make sure he is exercised regularly, I would be much appreciative."

"Of course, Clarissa?" He questioned, "Clarissa of the golden tresses and sky blue eyes?" He asked, his eyes sparking interest. "Your mother's maid, also known as the only woman you could ever love? That Clarissa was sent to retrieve you?"

"Please do not start, Fairchild."

"You only speak of her every time you are in your cups. Last night you waxed quite poetic about the sound of her laughter and her radiant smile." Fairchild went to the window, overlooking the avenue. He turned to David, with an eyebrow raised. "That is her, the little vision in the blue dress?"

David scowled at him. "Yes, that is Clarissa."

"Well, at least I know there is nothing wrong with your eyes. She is quite the lovely little thing, isn't she? Maybe I should go introduce myself," Fairchild said wolfishly.

"You do that and I will rescind the offer of my home while I am away. You would rather be trapped in your mansion with your mother and five sisters?" David threatened. Fairchild gave a visible shudder.

"I was only jesting, my friend. You know I am a married man," Fairchild protested. This time David raised an eyebrow. It was common knowledge that Fairchild hadn't laid eyes on his bride since the day after he married her nearly five years ago, and she had taken off for the continent, apparently only using the marriage as a means of escape from her overbearing father. At least that was the story Fairchild had always maintained. He suspected there was much more to it, but Fairchild, whose life was an open book, was surprisingly reticent about speaking about his marriage. David never pressed his friend on the issue, so he let the subject drop.

"I will send word, once I've reached Hollister House. I do not know when I will be back, to London." David told him. Fairchild did not seem displeased by the news. He probably was looking forward to the peace of living alone, something that David never quite got used to, himself. They gave their farewells and satisfied, he stepped out his front door, locking it behind him, wondering how long it would be before he was back.

Chapter Two

Coming out of the townhouse, Clarissa laid a hand to her stomach, trying to calm the butterflies that seemed to be swarming there now. It was the first time she'd laid eyes on David in several months. That visit had been cut short due to a row between him and the Duchess. When he confronted his mother with his suspicions that all his servants were reporting his activities back to her, after she angrily confirmed the allegations, he'd stormed out, and proceeded back to London where he let go of all of the servants in question. To Clarissa's knowledge, he never hired any replacements. That fact was quite evident by the state of the townhouse.

Of course, the Duchess had other ways to keep tabs on her son, and used those accordingly. For months now their only point of contact was through their man of business in London. His only reporting was a few investments that David had queried him about, and some small withdrawals from his account, that were well below what he had been going through before. It appeared he was trying to cut himself off financially from the Duchess, when in fact it was his money she was managing.

She and the Duchess had expected to see him home over the holidays, but he did not show. The Duchess had written him several times, but he never responded to any of her letters. Clarissa knew that the Duchess had alluded to her illness in the letters, but pride kept her from ever stating how dire her condition truly was.

Despite the ongoing battle between David, and his mother the Duchess, Clarissa blamed herself for their estrangement. She knew part of the reason David stayed away was because of her. He didn't want to be reminded of the mistake he'd nearly made so many years ago. A few days ago, the Duchess finally relented, wanting to put an end to the stand-off with David. She asked Clarissa to go to London, and retrieve her son. Clarissa hated London, and had gone out of her way to avoid any contact with David for years. Still, she would never refuse this request, for she knew it for what it really was an acknowledgement that she had little time left. The Duchess was going to die. It was time she put things right with her son.

With a heavy heart, Clarissa left on the journey, determined to bring David back, in chains, if necessary, no matter how much pain it cost her. To be honest, she had expected David to put up more of a fight. She was a bit stunned that he had capitulated so easily. She took a deep breath to steady herself and walked the few steps to the carriage. "Mac, we'll be leaving shortly. The Duke will be out in a few minutes," she told MacPherson, the longtime servant of the Duchess. He jumped down from his seat and opened the door for her, and handed her up into the carriage, where she would wait for David. Mac gave her a considering look.

"Are you feeling poorly, Miss Clarissa?" He asked in concern. She'd known MacPherson her entire life. He'd been a boy when he came to work for the Duke, David's father, before he had even married the Duchess. He had started out as a tiger on the estate, then head stable boy, now he ran the stable. He also trained the estate horses, and drove the carriage on the rare occasion that it was brought out. He'd even taught Clarissa and David how to ride when they were children. She thought of him as a surrogate uncle and appreciated his concern.

"I'm fine, Mac, it's been a rather long journey, and I'm a bit tired."

"May-haps we should stay the night in London, and get a fresh start at dawn on the morrow?" MacPherson suggested.

"No, it's already past noon now. As it is, it will be nightfall before we get to Glenburn. I'll be fine." She said, indicating the near the halfway point of their journey where the only inn worthy of Duke (or so the Duchess always claimed) stood.

It had been over three years since she'd made a trip to London. She accompanied the Duchess as her companion as she attended the festivities of the newly crowned Queen Victoria. It was the one and only time she had ever attended any ton events. The Duchess Drusilla bought her a beautiful gown to wear to the Queens Ball they'd attended. David was their escort. It was the first time she had seen him dressed formally, befitting his station, and it had taken her breath away that night. The carriage ride to the ball had been strained. She tried so hard not to look at him, but it seemed every time she looked up, she would find him looking at her, and she felt her face burn. She felt like he was a stranger. Not the boy she loved all her life.

He'd danced with his mother, then she watched as he danced with the young Queen, who was but a slip of a girl; younger than Clarissa by three years. The Duchess had been standing beside her. "Imagine if he married her, he could be the Royal Consort." The Duchess had said, in awe. The words had felt like a knife to Clarissa, because they were no exaggeration. It was indeed possible that the Queen could consider taking him to husband. He was a Duke; he was elevated enough to marry into royalty. Whereas to the world, Clarissa was a mere ladies' maid and companion to the Duchess, she could not compete with that. She didn't dare hope to.

It was in that moment that she truly realized how insane it was to assume that someday they'd be together. Despite everything, she had held out hope that someday, when David was ready to settle down, he would come back to her. Now she knew that could never be. The circumstances of their existence forbid it.

When David came to her later that evening to claim a waltz with her, she had been fraught with anxiety. He told her she looked lovely, she could not even reply to his compliment, just gave him a nod. She'd held herself stiffly in his arms and refused to look at him. He'd tried to draw her out, but even the most minimal small talk was beyond her. Finally, as the dance ended, he said bitterly, "I understand now. I'll not bother you again." He dropped her hands and walked away. In that moment she knew anything that they had, anything that they might have had was irrevocably gone.

Seeing him today, she was reminded of the boy she had grown up with, the one who was her best friend, her confidant. Who would walk with her hand and hand through the woods and spend hours gazing up at the sky from a tree house they had built together. He was the one who challenged her, and made her laugh and applauded even her smallest achievements. Whose lips had been the first to touch hers, whose hands had been the first to caress her, intimately, she missed that boy with an ache that never quite went away.

She reminded herself that boy was also the one who left her and shattered her heart and her trust. She'd never let him have that much power over her again. She was here for the Duchess, because she was dying and wanted to see her son. It was important that he be fully prepared to take over all of the entailment when he reached his twenty fifth birthdays in just over two months' time. She was there to honor a dying wish, not because she had any illusion that she and David would ever find their way back to each other, or that they were meant to be. She'd been disillusioned of that fact long ago. She was here at the behest of the Duchess and for no other reason. She just had to keep telling herself that.

Chapter Three

The ride to Glenburn was a tedious affair. At this time of year, the landscape was more gray than green, and as he knew every turn and sight by heart, there was nothing of true interest to look at, outside the windows of the carriage.

David instead focused his gaze on Clarissa where she sat across from him, she had taken her bonnet off some time ago, but her pale blonde hair was still restrained, pulled tight in a bun. Not lose or in a braid as she had usually worn it, since they were children. He supposed it was her ways of making herself look unapproachable. Little did she know that it just made him itch to unpin it, and set it loose. He sighed, he couldn't even let himself think the thought, and it was a sure path to misery.

It had been several hours since they left London, and dusk was approaching. They were still a few miles from the inn he frequented whenever he made his semi-annual trips to the estate. The stilted conversation between Clarissa and he had been exhausted hours ago, and she seemed relieved that he was no longer trying to talk to her. She was careful to keep every word impersonal and deferring to his station.

It would be late in the afternoon of the next day before they would reach their destination. At this rate, it would be one of the longest, most agonizing journeys of his life. Still, the fact that Clarissa had come alone; to bring him back told him that the situation was serious. He knew that she didn't care for London at all, and had gone to great lengths to not be alone with him in the last several years. Ever since that night...He shook his head as if to rid himself of the memory. No use going down that road. She silently stared out the window of the carriage, at the passing countryside, her expression pensive, solemn. She was clearly worried about his mother. He had no reason to doubt her devotion to the Duchess.

She had lived in the house since birth, and had taken over the duties of companion and ladies-maid to the Duchess, when her own mother, Annabelle, had passed away, nearly a decade earlier. They grew up together in the same household, had even shared a governess and been educated together until he went away to Eton when he was thirteen. He remembered those first few months away at school. He had missed his mother, of course, and Annabelle, who had been like a beloved aunt to him. But most of all, he had been homesick for Clarissa.

She had always been his best friend, his ally. He had longed to be with her, exploring the woods that ringed the estate or skipping stones across the surface of the lake. Even if she always seemed to best him at it, he missed that girl, the carefree, kind hearted girl with the sky blue eyes and the hair like sunshine, her ticklish laugh that echoed across the lake. This solemn woman across from him, no longer resembled that girl. He had to wonder how much of that his fault was.

His thoughts turned to their shared birthday coming up in two months' time. They would both be five and twenty. At twenty-five, he came into his full inheritance, all the entailed and unentailed properties would no longer be under the Duchess's stewardship, as outlined in his father's will. It would all be under his control. Would his mother even live to see that day? He hadn't seen her in months. It seemed every contact they had; she spent in criticism of his life, the drinking, the gambling, and the whoring. It all horrified her, as it should.

Over the last several months he had cut down on the gambling and the women. Truth be told, no feminine bodies had warmed his sheets in well over a year. He'd come to realize that the physical release was not worth the emptiness that filled him afterwards. He looked up at Clarissa. Another fault he could lay at her door. She looked up at him, catching him staring. He knew he should turn away but he wanted to reach through the facade and see the girl he remembered, again, needing her right now.

"Clary..." He whispered. He saw, for the briefest moment, the wall come down, at the mention of his childhood nickname for her. She had called him Davey then. No one else had ever called him that. Now he was Your Grace, or Hollister or Lord David to his familiars. But he longed to hear her call him Davey in that lilting, laughing voice of hers. He hadn't been Davey, to her, since he was sixteen. The first time she had called him Your Grace, the words had cut him, as they were meant to. Now he was numb to that pain, or so he thought. God, how was it possible to miss a person so much when they were right in front of him?

He opened his mouth to speak, but a noise outside the carriage grabbed his attention. The carriage came to a careening halt, and both he and Clarissa ended up on the floor. He caught her in his arms. A glance out the window told him that they were being forced to stop. He saw at least three men with scarves tied across the lower half of their faces and their hats pulled down low, all brandishing pistols. He felt fear clutch him. Is this what his father felt in his last moments?

Clarissa struggled to sit up but he forced her

flat on the floor. At all costs he had to protect her. She began to protest but he leaned down and whispered in her ear, "There are men out there with guns. Stay down." She nodded, and he could feel her shaking. He wanted nothing more than to lie there and hold her in his arms, but he knew he had to take action if he wanted to get them out of this alive. He reached to the secret compartment he knew that was under the seat and opened the latch.

Since the death of their fathers, the Duchess made certain that every conveyance the estate owned had an arsenal of weapons aboard. The Duchess herself had taught him, and Clarissa, how to shoot at the age of eight. It had always galled him that Clarissa was always the better shot, although he usually hit his target. Two pistols and a dagger lay in the compartment. He pulled everything out, and checked to see that the guns were both loaded. He handed one to Clarissa, and took one for himself, as well as the dagger. "If they get past me, you do what you need to do to defend yourself," he whispered in her ear. She nodded.

He started to get up, but she grabbed him by his jacket lapel and pulled him back to her. "Davey...I...be careful." She said, then much to his amazement, she kissed him. He felt it like a jolt of lightning to his system. When her lips pulled away she looked into his eyes "For luck," she said.

For a stunned moment, he did nothing, all his instincts wanted him to go back to her lips for more, but he knew he had to deal with the situation outside, keep Clarissa safe. That thought was his motivation.

He charged out of the carriage and with a war whoop, went after the first man, his dagger went straight into the man's thigh as he wheeled around on his horse, and he grabbed for the pistol in the man's hand and managed to pull him off the horse. One foot was caught in the stirrup. The man got a shot off, which missed David but hit the carriage. The horse startled and took off, dragging the screaming man through the woods. One man was off his horse and on top of the carriage fighting with MacPherson, the driver, who was nearly unconscious. David leveled his gun at the man and the moment he reared back to punch MacPherson yet again, David saw his shot and took it. The man fell like a stone, toppling from the carriage to the ground.

Just then he felt something hard pressed against the back of his head, and the sound of a gun cocking. "Well," the man said "at least now I won't have to worry about splitting my reward three ways." He braced himself for the shot he knew was about to come. Clarissa...at least Clarissa was safe, and he had felt her lips on his one last time...

The shot was loud and he felt a whoosh and

splatter of blood and tissue, rain over his back, and he staggered to his knees, feeling a weight and darkness...but no pain. Wasn't getting shot supposed to hurt? He shook his head. It was still moving. He frowned in confusion. Was he dead?

"David!" he heard Clarissa scream.

"Stay...stay back," he called to her; he tried to move, to get to her but something was keeping him down. He heard Clarissa grunting and scrabbling in the dirt. What was happening? Was the man hurting her? He couldn't see blood and matter clouded his eyes, "Clary..." he gasped. "Shoot him!"

"I did! I can't get him off of you. He weighs a ton," she exclaimed. "Help me."

It was then that he realized that he hadn't been shot at all, that Clarissa had shot his assailant. That it was that man's blood that covered him and his dead weight holding him down. Here he was, trying to protect her, and she had saved him.

Typical.

He heaved himself up on his hands and knees and then finally freed himself of the dead-weight of the body that had been atop his. He rolled over and lay on the ground, and blinked, trying to clear his head. His ears were still ringing from the gunshot that had been so close to his own head. He felt a cloth dab at his face and wipe his eyes. He blinked to look up and see Clarissa leaning over him as she tried to clean him with a torn bit of her slip. He reached up and caressed her face. She smiled at him and he grinned back. His hand went to the back of her head and he felt something warm and sticky, and frowned. "Clary?" he said, and then brought his hand back, so that they could both see it covered in blood,

"Oh...Davey... I've been shot," she said as her eyes rolled back in her head, and for the second time that day, David found himself under an unconscious body.

Chapter Four

Lord Grey checked his pocket watch for the hundredth time in the last three hours, and tried to stifle the feeling of unease. He shouldn't have paid the men anything up front. A hundred pounds he'd handed over, with the promise of nine hundred more once the deed was done. Still, a hundred pounds was a considerable sum to the renegades, if they disappeared after that, it wouldn't be surprising.

A commotion in front of the inn caught his attention. A carriage bearing the Hollister insignia had come to a stop in front of the building, the heaving horses, stamping and throwing their heads in agitation. A dark haired man leaped down from the jump board. He was heavily splattered in blood. Behind him, he saw MacPherson, or who he thought was MacPherson, struggle off the board, and landed heavily on the ground, his face was a swollen mass of bruises and oozing blood. The dark haired man was shouting for help, for a doctor and a constable. He threw open the door of the carriage and pulled out a blond girl, slight in frame, blood ran freely from a wound at the crown of her head.

Grey cursed. This had to be the Duke, David, and the maid that the Duchess Drusilla had sent to retrieve him. He hadn't seen David, since he was a boy-the day he had been dropped off at Eton, and even then it had been from afar. People were scurrying about, and orders were being shouted. The man refused to hand over the girl, and insisted on carrying her up the stairs to a room, himself. MacPherson was being helped into the inn, and people cleared a bench for him to lie down. It was only a matter of minutes before the town surgeon came in, bearing a heavy leather bag and was directed straight up the stairs, the constable right behind him.

Grey kept his head down, but he cocked his head to hear what was being said, and blatantly listened as MacPherson gave his account of the men that accosted them, and the events. Two men were dead, that he knew of. The third stabbed and run off into the woods.

Grey cursed. Imbeciles! How could they have messed this up? All they had to do was stopping the carriage and kill its occupants. Twenty-five years ago he had hired men from the same gang of ruffians, to take care of Duke Dorian, and it had gone smoothly. Of course, things hadn't gone completely as planned on that venture, years ago, either. Lady Drusilla was supposed to have been on the carriage that time, but hadn't made the trip. She went into mourning and never left the estate, he had visited one time before the birth and that had gone disastrously.

In hindsight, he knew he had handled that visit badly. Declaring that he was the new Duke and demanding that the obviously pregnant Duchess Drusilla leave the premises had been a bad move on his part and only infuriated the Duchess. He feared it had turned her suspicion towards him. She had summarily had him removed from the premises. He had ordered MacPherson, who was the stable boy at the time, to notify him the moment Drusilla gave birth, and he had waited. Three months later, the boy arrived on his doorstep, and he had demanded to know if it was a boy or girl and the perplexed boy stuttered he didn't know-didn't think to ask before coming. He'd been well into his cups on that night but could not stay away, he had to know. He had to go to the estate himself and had to fight off a couple of footman to get upstairs to the Duchess's suite.

He had convinced himself the babe would be a female and had plans of pushing the babe and mother out the door that night-no one would stop him. When he had pulled the swaddling off the baby to see that it was a boy, red fury had clouded his vision. This squalling brat had stolen his title, his inheritance. He wasn't even aware that he had raised his fist, just knew he would not let this thing steal what was rightfully his, that he had to get rid of it. The pain of the poker cracking through the bone of his arm brought him out of his anger filled stupor. She had shouted him down and then he was physically removed from the property and never allowed back.

The next day he received papers from a barrister, stating that he had to maintain a distance of no less than fifty miles from the estate and Duchess Drusilla and, as he found out, the infant David George Dorian Thoroughgood, Duke of Hollister. Along with it were copies of Dorian's will, showing his desire that in the event of his death, Duchess Drusilla control all of the estate holdings until his progeny reached their 25th birthday. In return, he would get his own estate, with paid staff and a quarterly stipend. If he was caught violating the agreement, he would lose it all.

She held the purse strings, but he found ways to get around it. He received monthly missives from MacPherson, although most of the time those were useless. He wrote of things like new rose bushes being planted in the garden or horses foaling in the stable. When the boy David, had gone off to Eton and then Cambridge, he received stiff reminders that he was not allowed to be within fifty miles of either of those areas. When David moved to London, he had been banned from there as well. He was sure if Drusilla could have walled him into the estate that he had been banished to, she would have.

A month ago he had left his estate, telling the estate manager he was heading towards Bath on an extended holiday, but instead he went to stay at an inn two towns over from Hollister Estates. He had registered under an assumed name, and grown his beard thick, and wore a pair of thick spectacles, certain that Lady Drusilla, nor anyone else, would ever recognize him after all this time. He did this knowing that nearing his twenty fifth birthday, David would be required to come home soon, to take over the running of the estate, as well as the rest of the entailed holdings. Then he began the great wait, and contacted MacPherson, and arranged a meeting with him twice a week, to keep apprised of Duke David's comings and goings. When MacPherson had revealed a few days ago, that they were going to London to retrieve David, and expected to come right back with him-due to Duchess Drusilla's illness, he saw his chance. He contacted the same man who had taken care of Duke Dorian, years earlier. The man had rounded up his nephew and a cousin and the plan went into motion.

Grey had hated handing over the money to the reprobate. The amount was equivalent to his whole quarterly stipend, but he suspected they wouldn't dare take on the job without some cash up front. They were supposed to meet him here, when it was over, and he would hand over the rest of the money. Then they would part company. His pocket was still heavy with the roll of ten pound notes.

Now he knew that plan had failed abysmally, plus there was no way to get his hundred pounds back. That thought aggravated him the most. He hated when plans fell apart. Setting his hat firmly on his head, he strode over to MacPherson, where he lay on the bench, groaning in pain. He tapped the man on the shoulder and was rewarded when he opened a slit of an eye and recoiled in horror. He bent down so that he could whisper in MacPherson's ear. "Remember, Mac, my boy, if I swing, you swing. Meet me in two days at the usual place and time. And if you tell anyone, your pretty Betty and your boy, will pay."

He strode out the door, and rounded to the back of the Inn, where his horse was waiting. He stopped in his tracks as he beheld Duke David, not ten feet away from him. He had two large buckets of water next to him, and while Grey watched, he upended one over his head, fully clothed. Tracks of blood sluiced down his face and neck and the darkly stained shirt. A puddle of blood tinged water now lay at his feel. He poured the second bucket over his head, which ran clearer. Dropping the buckets to the ground, he bent over, bracing his shaking hands against his thighs and took in several deep breaths, dripping,

dripping, for several minutes. Grey didn't dare move though he was certain that David didn't even realize he was there, so lost in the aftermath of the trauma.

"She's alive," he heard David whisper. "She's alive. She's alive. That's all that matters." Straightening, David reached for a towel he'd slung over a nearby post and vigorously dried himself off. He visibly shuddered when he pulled the towel away and it was somewhat tinged in pink.

Grey's hand curled around the handle of the revolver he had in the inside of his jacket. He could end this right this instant, and it would all be his. He glanced around, there were at least two men within sight in the stable, and a kitchen maid was coming out of the inn now, bearing a pail of scraps, which she proceeded to dump into a trough for the pigs kept in a pen not far away. Too many witnesses, plus getting his own hands dirty, had never been his style.

Reluctantly, he relaxed his grip from around the handle and just then, David looked up, right at him. They eyed each other warily, but Grey saw no sign of recognition in his eyes, just distrust. He could hardly blame the boy, considering what he'd been through. Grey gave him a reassuring smile.

"I saw you come in. Seems like you had a bit of trouble, is your lady well?" Grey asked.

"We were accosted by highwaymen and they shot and grazed her. She's still unconscious, but the surgeon seems to think she will be alright, once she comes to. Are you from around here?" he asked. Grey shook his head.

"No...a traveler, like yourself. I shudder to think it could have been me, those highwaymen came after I would have made a handier target, an old man traveling alone. But they could probably see I wouldn't have had the coin to spare. Still, it is tragic this happened to you. I shall pray you and your lady complete your journey in safety."

"Thank you sir, I appreciate that. Safe travels to you as well" David said sincerely. He swung the towel over his shoulder and tipped his head in salute, and walked back into the back door of the inn.

Lord Grey collected his horse, and thought briefly about lying in wait, just outside of town to try again, to kill David, then just as quickly, rejected that thought. He'd been patient for twenty-five years, what were a few more days or weeks, in the scheme of things? He wasn't giving up. His opportunity would come again. He'd waited twenty-five years to make this right. He just had to be patient. His time would come. When the estate came to him, he wanted no question that he was the rightful Duke, and everything would be his.

Chapter Five

Clarissa struggled to open her eyes. Her head throbbed, and she frowned. Reaching up she encountered a thick bandage covering her scalp. She tried to focus. The room was mostly dark, except for a lamp burning next to the bed, which was turned down low. She saw David in a rocking chair just a few feet away; his head slumped at an angle that had to be uncomfortable. She turned her head to look around the room but the movement caused a jarring of pain in her skull and she gasped out loud. Instantly David startled awake. He looked confused for a moment but that cleared. He leaned forward and took her hand.

"Are you back with us, Clary?" He asked, gently.

"What happened?" she asked. He frowned.

"What do you remember?"

"I'm not sure. I...there were men with guns, they made the carriage stop. A gun went off and something hit the back of my head, a rock or something."

"My dear Clary, that rock was a bullet." He explained gently. "Luckily you were grazed, but you have quite a gouge at the crown of your head. You may have to style your hair a bit differently for a while, the doctor shaved around the wound area to clean it. You may have a bit of a concussion too. How does the head feel?"

"Like someone shot it, how do you think?" She answered grumpily, and he chuckled.

"There's the old Clary I remember." He clasped her hand tighter in his, and she knew she should pull her hand away, but didn't have the will. She closed her eyes, and she remembered the sight of that man with his gun against the back of David's head. She'd been so terrified, just reliving that moment had her shaking now. If she had missed, if he had pulled the trigger first…suddenly there wasn't enough air in the room, she felt herself gasping. She clutched at David. He was alright. He had to be alright. "Clary…sweetheart, what's happening? Breathe for me," he said. He climbed into the bed with her and pulled her into a sitting position. He wrapped his arms around her and pulled her close to his body.

"H…he was going to k..kill…you." She stammered and burst into tears.

"But he didn't. You saved me. I'd wring your neck for risking yourself for me if I weren't so grateful to be alive," he said stroking her back, her face.

"Y..You're a...alive," she hiccupped. He nodded.

"I am. I was not hurt at all, I promise."

"I killed him."

"In self-defense or my defense, you were very brave," he assured her.

"I'm not feeling brave right now."

"That's just how you are Clary. Just like my mother. Calm in a crisis and falling to pieces the moment all the smoke clears."

"Will I have to go to trial for killing that man?" she asked, in fear of the answer. David shook his head.

"I've already dealt with it. The local constable has been and gone. You and I acted in self-defense and no charges will be brought, on either of us."

"Where are we?"

"Glenburn, The Red Owl Inn, a few miles, from where the incident occurred."

"How did I get here? I remember wiping the blood from your face and then...waking up here.

"You fainted. Keeled right over, and frightened the life out of me, I may add. I wasn't sure of the extent of your injury, then. I threw you into the carriage and shoved MacPherson aside and drove the horses to exhaustion to get here. Luckily the village sports a surgeon and a constable."

"MacPherson," she exclaimed, "is he hurt?"

"Broken nose and blackened eyes. He's a sad sight but he'll be fine. A few days of Betty's coddling and he'll be good as new, I'm sure." He assured her. "I think it best if we delay going back a day, so you and he can heal a bit before we get back on the road."

She wanted to argue with him, but the idea of being jostled around in the carriage so soon made her queasy, so she just nodded. One extra day, the Duchess would understand. Oh, she dreaded having to tell her of what happened. She was in such a delicate state and she didn't want to upset her. They would have to underplay the enormity of the event. She hoped their acting skills were up to the task.

"Are you feeling better now?" he asked, still stroking her back. She suddenly realized their position. He was in bed with her, his arms around her, she was draped over him. This was highly inappropriate. She froze at once and tried to pull away.

"Don't, please don't Clary. Just lay here with me. You may not need this, but I do," he said quietly. She stilled in his arms.

"The Duchess would not be pleased to know we were in the same bedchamber...in the same bed," she whispered.

"No...I imagine she would not, but she isn't here, and I won't tell, if you won't." He said. She smiled against his chest. How many times had they both said that when they were children? There had been a time when he had held all her secrets, and she had held his. When it seemed they shared one soul, one heart between them. He lay back and pulled the covers over them.

"Do you remember the thunderstorms?" he whispered. She nodded and felt the tears prickle her eyes. She'd always been frightened of storms, especially at night. As a small child at the first crack of lightning, she would scurry to David's room and climb into his bed, and he would wrap his arms around her and she had felt...safe. After he went away to school, she had lain in her bed and cried during the first storm. She had missed him so much, and been so afraid. Over the years, the pain of his being gone just became a dull ache that never quite went away. Every time he had come home on holiday, he seemed less and less like the boy she had worshiped and loved, and turned into this other being, who was more concerned with his status and the status of his friends than with her. She closed her eyes against that, not wanting to think of the painful time.

"I miss thunderstorms, with you," David said. "Every time it rains at night, I think of you," he admitted.

"I think of you, too," she said, he hugged her close, and she knew it wasn't sexual, she relaxed.

"I almost lost you, today, Clary. I can't lose you. Not again," he whispered against her ear. She felt a tear trickle against her cheek and she realized it was his. She started to cry, they had caused each other so much pain. But what was there for them, except pain?

"Davey...I can't." She whispered brokenly.

"I know. I've just felt so...lost, these years, without you. I just need you in my arms tonight. I need to not feel lost, just this one night." he pleaded in a whisper. She nodded. She needed it too. Just this one night, she needed to feel the other part of her soul, the other side of her heart, together. She felt him relax, his breathing slow. She drifted off to sleep, feeling safe and secure and with a sad smile on her lips.

Chapter Six

David awoke, the bed empty. Looking up, he spied Clarissa at the vanity mirror. She had taken her bandage off and was holding a hand mirror at an awkward angle behind her head, trying to get a look at the gaping wound left behind. She frowned at the mirror "Did they really need to shave so much away? I'll have to take to wearing bonnets indoors," she grumbled, aloud. David chuckled and she spun around to the bed. He saw the moment; the wall went up. She straightened and averted her eyes. Damn it!

"Oh, I'm sorry, Your Grace, I didn't mean to wake you," she apologized. He sighed, so she was back to Your Gracing him again. He should have known it wouldn't last.

"Clary..."

"Please...I am feeling much better, just a slight headache. I think we should continue our journey today," she insisted. Her mouth was set and she was avoiding his penetrating gaze. She was in full retreat mode, now. Last night, he had her back, his Clary. For a few hours, they had lain in each other's arms and talked. Easing the empty feeling he had carried inside for so long. Now that empty feeling was back, and with it, the crushing pain. He wanted to weep. He wanted to hurl something and rage at her for closing him out, yet again. But he did none of that. Instead he nodded stoically.

"Of course," He got out of the bed and pulled his boots on. "I'll have them send up a bath, and breakfast to you. I will let MacPherson know to have the horses readied. Will an hours' time suffice?"

"Yes, that would be fine. Thank you, Your Grace," she said softly. His hand was on the door knob and he froze, and leaned his forehead against the jam and took a steadying breath.

"You break my heart, Clary." He said his voice husky with pain.

He opened the door and went through, pulling it shut behind him. But not before he heard her reply "As you break mine."

David strode down the stairs, and ordered that a bath and food be brought up to Clarissa. He then made his way out to the stable; MacPherson had slept there, last night, with the carriage. He roused him, and together they readied the horses.

He'd known MacPherson his entire life. During his youth, in a household full of women he would often seek solace in the stables. He and MacPherson would talk of manly things. Mac would often tell him stories of his life from when he had started off as a tiger to his father and been mentored by George, Clarissa's father. It was quite evident that he had adored George and the Duke, Dorian, and his stories made both of the men seem very real. Mac had graduated from tiger to stable hand, and now he ran the stable and was often their coach driver on the rare occasion that his mother, the Duchess Drusilla, ever left Hollister House. MacPherson was perhaps a dozen years older than himself, but his weathered features made him look much older. And now, with both his eyes blackened and his face bruised and swollen he looked quite haggard. "I can drive the team today, Mac." David offered, "You can ride in the coach, you're in no shape to be driving."

"No, Your Grace, I can do it," Mac insisted.

"You taught me yourself how to ride a horse and drive a team. I know what I'm doing. I'll be fine. Plus, you can keep an eye on Miss Clarissa for me. She insists she is fine and ready for travel but I suspect she is but putting on a brave face."

"Aye…yes, I can watch the girl. I vowed that day that both your fathers passed I'd watch over the both of you. I'll not be shirking my responsibilities now," Mac promised.

"I thought of them yesterday, when the incident happened. I thought it was so like the story you'd told me as a boy, of how my father and

Clarissa's father died. I thought for a few brief moments we'd follow the same fate," David admitted.

"As did I, Your Grace. I had a horror of history repeating itself. I am sorry, I did not see them sooner, or try to outrun them. I was driving along and suddenly they were upon us. The one who went after me had quite the left hook; I think one more blow would have done me in. If you had not taken a bullet to him when you did, I would have been finished, I know. I do thank you, Your Grace. I thank God that I did not bring my boy, Robbie, with me."

"I only wish I had gotten to him sooner. I, myself was saved by Miss Clarissa. I am quite lucky that she is still the best shot at Hollister. So tell me, how is Robbie? It's been ages since I've seen him."

"Aye, my Robbie's grown like a weed, sixteen and almost a head taller than myself. He helps me in the stables, and is quite handy. I think he's even better with the horses than I am. I left him in charge of the stables while Miss Clarissa and I came to London. Your mare Persephone is about to foal. Robbie's helped me deliver every foal over the last ten years. I thought I'd give him the chance to deliver one on his own, though to be honest Persephone will do most of the work. He's a fine boy, my Robbie. I couldn't be prouder." MacPherson bragged.

David felt a moment of envy. Would his own father have been proud of him? Perhaps not with the way he had been acting, avoiding Hollister House and his mother in the last several months. Gambling and drinking to excess when he should have already taken over the reins from the duchess, and been well on his way to handling his own affairs.

He was less than two months from his twenty fifth birthdays, when he would officially meet his majority and the entirety of his family fortune, as well as all of the ducal duties would be his. No matter his mother's condition, he should have been back to Hollister House well before now. He had time to make up for, and a need to prove himself to his mother, before it was too late.

As they finished harnessing the horses, the constable showed up. Letting them know that they had found the third man, the one that David had stabbed in the thigh and fallen from his horse. He'd been dragged a few miles from the sight of the attack, and had been found with a broken neck. David could not summon up an ounce of remorse. That man was the one whose bullet had grazed Clarissa. If his aim had been any truer, she would have been killed. Even now, the thought left him cold. He could not fathom a world without Clarissa in it.

David knew if he had come home of his own volition, Clarissa would never have had to come to London to retrieve him. She would not have been there. Although he had no idea why those men had accosted him yesterday, he had to own his own part in what had happened to Clarissa and to MacPherson. It had been his own stubbornness that had brought this down on them as surely as it had been the highwayman or whoever was behind them. It was a most sobering thought.

He had exiled himself away from Hollister House, his mother, and his ducal responsibilities, because to be near Clarissa, to see her, and not have her, was a pain he could not bear.

If yesterday taught him one thing, it was that being around her was not nearly as unbearable as the idea of her death. No matter what, even if he could not have her, he wanted her to be happy. That meant more to him than anything, and if he could help her find happiness, even if it was not with him, he would do everything in his power to make it happen.

Chapter Seven

Clarissa looked out the window of the carriage and could see the rising stone spires of the estate coming up, around the bend. She took a deep breath, and again swallowed down the nausea that had been plaguing her for the last few hours, home at last. Soon enough she'd be on solid ground, and could go to bed. She reached across to where MacPherson, lay on the seat and gently shook him awake. "Mac, we are at the gates of the Hollister House." She told him. He groaned and she felt bad. The man had taken quite a beating to the face and could barely see through the slits of his blackened eyes. She was certain he was in much pain and the jostling of the carriage hadn't helped. David had insisted on driving in his stead, and she had been relieved to know she did not have to spend several awkward hours in his company. It probably would have been wise to rest and extra day, before finishing their travel. As it was, her head raged and the constant motion had left her feeling quite queasy.

Once she was on solid ground again, she'd be fine, she told herself.

The carriage stopped in the circular drive in front of the house. She waited as a footman put down the step. She insisted MacPherson precede her, and he did not argue. She needed a moment to pull herself together. She really did not feel well at all. David stuck his head in the door of the carriage. "Coming?" he asked, then frowned, seeing her pallor. "Are you all right?"

"Yes of course. I'm fine," she lied.

She stepped out of the carriage, accepting his hand, as she descended the steps. The moment her foot hit the ground she bent over and immediately emptied the contents of her stomach on the ground. She felt David's hands, one come around her waist to support her, the other rubbing her back. She was simultaneously comforted and mortified.

"Oh Clary, you're not fine at all," he murmured. When it seemed there was nothing left to purge, she felt weak and shaky. She didn't protest as David swept her up in his arms. She was vaguely aware of footmen scurrying about them, retrieving their bags from the carriage.

David ordered Franklin, the butler to send for a physician, and have tea brought up to her room. He then proceeded to carry her upstairs, and did not stop until he deposited her on her bed. Betty MacPherson, the upstairs maid was beside herself.

"Miss Clarissa, whatever happened?" she asked. Before she could reply, David answered.

"We had an altercation yesterday with some highwaymen." He told her. "Betty, I'm afraid Mac was roughed up a bit, too. He'll be fine, but I'm sure he'll want some of your attention now. Go. I've got Miss Clarissa." He insisted.

Betty hesitated, torn briefly between staying to assist her employer and her husband. Finally, she curtsied and quickly made her leave.

David sat down on the edge of the bed and brushed the few damp tendrils away from her face "Tea will be up soon. I am so sorry, Clarissa, I should have insisted we wait another day to travel," he said with knowing regret.

"No...you were right, but we are here now. I'll be fine." If only her head would quit pounding and the room would quit spinning.

"What's going on here? David, what's happened?" A thin, thready voice said from the bedroom doorway. There stood the Duchess, clutching her dressing gown around her skeletal frame. Clarissa heard David gasp at the first sight of his mother. She felt bad, she should have warned him. The Duchess hardly resembled the vibrant woman she once was; her body a mere shell of its former self, her cheeks sunken in.

"Your Grace, you shouldn't be out of bed. I'm fine," Clarissa insisted closing her eyes again as the room seemed to resume spinning.

"Mother, I am handling this." David told her. "Please go back to bed, I'll be in shortly and tell you what happened."

"It's not proper for you to be here, in Clarissa's bedchamber. Where's Betty? " the Duchess insisted. David threw up his hands, and stood up, facing off with his mother.

"Betty is attending to her husband, who I dare say is in worse shape, now please, Mother. I promise you, Clarissa is safe from my advances. It is not my habit to be ravishing sickly women. Let me take care of her and I'll be in to see you, shortly."

Instead of leaving, she came to the bed and sat down, taking Clarissa's hand. Clarissa felt a soft touch, brushing her hair back from her cheek. She opened her eyes to see the Duchess worried green eyes, examining her closely, and a look of deep concern on her face. David stood stiffly at her side, his arms folded, clearly agitated with his mother, but at the same time, respecting her right to be there.

"What happened?" the duchess asked again. David's face wore a mutinous expression, but he answered her.

"Highwaymen, late yesterday, they stopped the coach, and meant to kill us. But we took care of them. Unfortunately, in the process, MacPherson was beaten up rather badly, and Clarissa... well, she took a bullet graze to the head, which left her concussed. I had a surgeon see to her right away, when it happened. I also had Franklin send for your physician as soon as we got here." He explained.

"Highwaymen? Dear lord, like the day My Dorian and George were...You could have both been killed!" The Duchess exclaimed, horrified.

"We were not, rest assured, Mother. Now please, let me escort you back to your room and let Clarissa rest." The duchess opened her mouth to protest, and then, apparently, thought better of it. She stood up and swayed alarmingly. David grabbed her before she could collapse to the floor.

For the second time that day he swung a woman up in his arms. He frowned in consternation. She weighed nearly nothing, and he could feel her bones through her dressing gown. He strode, purposely, down the hall towards the east wing where his mother's suite was located. "Put me down, David. I can walk." She protested feebly.

"Don't be ridiculous. It's just a bit further." Thankfully, she had left the door to her room ajar. He pushed it open, with a foot, walking through her sitting room to her bedchamber, depositing her on the edge of the bed. He looked around for a ladies' maid, before he remembered that Clarissa usually filled that position. He knelt in front of her and carefully unknotted the robe and drew it off her shoulders. He could clearly see she was nothing but skin and bones. And where her left breast should be, the night rail lay flat. A wave of alarm, and panic swept over him. She really was dying.

"Mother..." he choked.

"I'm sorry you have to see me like this. There is much we need to discuss and I fear there isn't much time left," she said. "Whether you think so or not, I am happy to see you, my dear boy," she told him.

He felt at once like a child, and now very, very old. He wasn't ready for this. No matter their differences, he did not want to lose her. He knelt in front of her and placed his head in her lap. She stroked her fingers through his hair. "You need a haircut." She said. He laughed through a sigh. Even in their most tender moments it seemed she would find fault. He chose to let it go.

"I will see to it tomorrow," he promised. He stood and helped her get under the covers. The duchess looked impossibly frail and small, her complexion nearly as pale as the sheets.

"I will be here tomorrow to see it, I assure you. Now go, and take care of our Clarissa. The girl is most precious to me."

"And to me," he stated quietly. She searched his face and sighed at what she found there.

"So that hasn't changed?"

"How could it? She's...Clarissa." He knew his mother didn't approve, but still, he wished for her understanding. He saw in her eyes, she did understand, only too well, and it saddened her.

"Go, attend her. I will see you in the morning." She said. He turned to go, then stopped and came back to the bed, and kissed his mother tenderly on the forehead. She reached up and patted him on the cheek, then closed her eyes. "Take care of our girl," she said, as she drifted off to sleep.

He passed his mothers' night nurse in the hall and let her know the Duchess was resting.

He made it back to Clarissa's room to see tea had been delivered. He dismissed the maid, insisting he could handle it. The maid curtsied and made her leave. He poured a cup for Clarissa, adding a dollop of cream and a generous spoonful of sugar. Exactly the way she liked it. He sat on the edge of the bed and helped her sit up. "There now, this will make you feel a bit better, I think." She took a sip, and another.

"Is the Duchess all right? It had to upset her, seeing me like this."

"She'll be fine. You know, she thrives on worry. I saw her to bed, and she drifted right off. We promised to talk in the morning."

"Good. I'm sure she is relieved that you are here."

"Yes...I'm sorry I wasn't here, sooner, of my own volition. You shouldn't have had to come to

London, to drag me home. I'm sorry I've been so stubborn, that I stayed away so long."

"That's in the past. You're here now. That's all that matters."

"I realize you were left to handle so much, it can't have been easy," he admitted.

"No. It hasn't been. But let's not dwell on that. No good can come of it. You are here, now, where you belong," she said as a discreet knock on the door, sounded.

"Your Grace, the physician is here," Franklin said from the doorway, leading a well-dressed young man into the room. The man inclined his head in deference to David.

"Your Grace, a pleasure to meet you. I am Doctor Reginald Bishop. I've been caring for your mother," he said, pulling his gloves off, he glanced towards the bed. "But I see it's Cissy who needs my attention today." He stepped around David and went to Clarissa.

Cissy? What the hell?

"Reggie... I'm fine. You didn't need to come," Clarissa said, sitting up. Her hand immediately went to her head. David stepped forward, not liking the familiarity between the two, and then stopped. The man was their physician, and of course Clarissa would know him well.

"I'll be the judge of that. What happened?"

"I was shot in the head," Clarissa told him, then had the audacity to giggle. She stopped quickly, realizing that laughing only hurt her head. The doctor sat on the bed and had Clarissa lean forward, to examine the wound.

"Aye, you have quite a gouge there, young lady. It's no wonder your head is hurting. I have a few powders you can take that will ease your pain. However, I think the best thing is rest. I see no signs of infection, keep the wound clean, and douse it with spirits every day until it closes up. I'm afraid you may have a bare spot there, for the rest of your days, but a bit of rearranging the part of your tresses should cover that up, no worries." He told her. He reached into his bag and pulled out a salve and carefully spread it over the wound and recovered the dressing. He spied her tea cup and poured an envelope of powder into the remaining tea and insisted Clarissa drink it.

She took a sip. "Oh, this is vile," she said, pushing the cup away.

"Cissy, I'm the physician here. I know it's vile. But it will take away the pain and help you sleep. Drink it up." He pushed the cup back and she glared at him, but did as he asked. Reginald put his supplies away in his bag, and it was obvious the powder was having an immediate effect on Clarissa. David came to stand next to Reginald at the side of her bed and she tilted her head back and grinned hazily up at both of them.

"Two handsome men in my bedchamber, I think I am ruined. I shall have to marry you both," she slurred, "Lucky me."

The doctor shared an amused look with David. He gave Clarissa a reassuring pat on the hand. "We shall keep this our secret, your virtue is safe from scrutiny," Reginald assured her. She sighed.

"I hold so many secrets; I think I shall burst with them someday," she murmured sadly, as her eyes drifted shut. David pulled the blankets up to her chin and straightened the covers.

"Your Grace, while I am here, I'd like to go have a look at the Duchess, then if we may have a word...privately," the doctor said.

"Of course, I shall meet you in the library at your convenience." The doctor nodded and exited the room. David was reluctant to leave Clarissa's side, but it was evident she was deeply asleep, and likely to remain so for hours. He silently left the room, shutting the door behind him. Stopping at his bedchamber, he took a few minutes to wash up and pulled on clean clothes. The day before he had made do with dousing himself with few buckets of cold water to rinse away the blood, behind the inn, as the surgeon had tended to Clarissa.

He still shuddered, remembering the stream of bloody water coming off of his body and pooling at his feet. He promised himself tomorrow he would take a nice long soak and have Franklin trim his hair. He wondered if one of the footmen might be moved up to be his valet. If he was going to be staying for any length of time he imagined, he would need one.

Before leaving his room, he glanced longingly at his bed. It had been a very long day, and he felt he could sleep for a week, but knew he should talk to the doctor regarding his mothers' health, and also to find out the extent of his relationship with Clarissa. He stilled at that thought. Was it his business if Clarissa had a tendre for the doctor? He seemed like a nice enough fellow and Clarissa was a woman of four and twenty. Well old enough to make her own decisions regarding her romantic liaisons. Yet the idea of Clarissa in the doctor's arms or anyone else's, filled him with a sense of despair he did not want to confront.

Chapter Eight

He took the stairs down to the main floor and followed the hall to the library. Stepping inside, he realized the room had not changed at all in the years, since he was a child, with the exception. There were many more books lining the shelves. A huge fireplace with an elaborately carved mantle took up most of one wall, and over it, hung his parents wedding portrait. He poured himself a drink and moved to stand in front of the portrait.

His mother was the same age as he was now in this picture, he thought, his father, a few years older. He had spent many an hour gazing at this painting, at the man that had died before he was born, and at the woman whose smile never quite reached her beautiful green eyes in the same way as they did within this image. He tried to see it, how he fit with these people. The Duchess had been so beautiful, her auburn hair set in an elaborate crown of ringlets. His father's hair was straight and pale blond, and pulled back in a queue. He had brilliant blue eyes that sparkled with merriment, and a half smirking smile-as if saying "Isn't it ridiculous that we have to pose for this silly portrait?" He could relate to that sentiment. When he was young he used to come into this room and study his father's face, and then study his own in a looking glass. He could not figure out why his father's familiar face, looked nothing like himself.

His mother had made him sit for portraits when he was turned six, and then again at sixteen. The only thing that had made it bearable was that Clarissa also had her portrait painted at the same time. The Duchess had said it was a gift for Annabelle, both times. He knew that his own portraits hung along the gallery wall, along with paintings of his parents and ancestors. He wasn't sure where Clarissa's portraits were. He'd have to search the attic and see if he could find them.

A knock sounded on the door of the library. "Dr. Reginald Bishop is here to speak with you, Your Grace," Franklin announced. David nodded and indicated that he be shown in. Reginald Bishop strode in. Franklin closed the door behind him.

"Can I get you a drink Doctor Bishop?" he asked.

"Certainly, whatever you are having there is fine," Reginald nodded. David poured him a brandy and handed it to him. They proceeded to the two armchairs in front of the fire. Reginald looked up at the painting over the fireplace.

"Are those your parents?" he asked. "Silly question, of course, I would recognize the Duchess anywhere."

"Yes, their wedding portrait."

Reginald studied the picture, and frowned, then looked appraisingly at David then back at the portrait again. "Not much of a family resemblance is there?" he stated.

David shrugged, "I'm told I look like my maternal grandfather, or so my mother says. I never met the man, and sadly no portraits exist of him that I know of."

"I remember studying about hereditary factors at University. It isn't uncommon to inherit traits from many generations past, whether it is eye color or disease."

"Do you think that is what happened with my mother? She inherited this disease? I know that her own mother passed when she was just a girl. She had a twin sister too; who died very young, although I understand that was from pleurisy." David asked.

"I've spoken to the Duchess regarding her family history. I believe that in this case there may be hereditary factors, sad to say. If she had a daughter I would warn her to guard her own health, carefully. You should remember that, if you have daughters, that they be told to take care with examinations of the breast, as the earlier it is detected, the better chance that it can be removed completely. I fear in this instance we did not discover it soon enough." The doctor said frankly, taking a long sip of his brandy. He set his glass down carefully, and looked David in the eye. "You know Her Grace had been feeling poorly for quite a while. She came to me about six months ago, after finding a mass. I thought it best to excise the breast, in an effort to contain the sickness. Sadly, at that point it was too late. She has been in steady decline ever since."

"Can nothing be done? No tonics or treatments? I've heard of healing baths on the continent. Would we be able to take her there?" David asked.

Reginald shook his head. "I am most sorry Your Grace; I regret to tell you that this is not something from which your mother will recover. She has not much time, a matter of weeks, perhaps a few months at best."

"Weeks! That cannot be. She was up, I saw her up, and walking earlier. Surely she has more time than that?"

"I know I spoke to the duchess while examining her a while ago, she told me of her little jaunt to Miss Cissy's bedside. I can assure you, that under most circumstances she would have not been able to take more than a few steps. I can only say her motivation was such that she was able to accomplish the task out of sheer determination."

"My mother is a most strong and determined woman. She's run this estate and all its holdings for years. One would hesitate to ever call woman the weaker sex after meeting my mother," David said dryly, with a hint of admiration. "That being said, doesn't will have a role in her health, and the time she has left?"

"Certainly, Your Grace. I do not underestimate the will of your mother; in fact I would say most women facing this would have already been buried in her stead. She has outlasted my initial hopes. Please know the stores of her energy are diminishing. I feel the only reason she has held this long was her desire to see you. I understand Miss Clarissa had to fetch you from London," the doctor said reprovingly.

David bristled, but he conceded that the good doctor was in fact, quite correct. He wouldn't be here now if Clarissa hadn't shown up, and forced him to return home. As he thought of her lying upstairs, he still felt ashamed she had needed to do that.

"I can assure you, I was unaware of my mother's true condition, or I would have been here much sooner. The fault is mine, as we have been estranged for some time."

"I had heard as much from Her Grace, and from Miss Clarissa, who has taken over the running of the estate in the last months of the duchess' decline."

"She has? I was not aware…"

"There seems to be a number of things that you are unaware of, Your Grace," Reginald claimed.

David gave him a narrow eyed gaze. "I'm sure you would like to enlighten me."

"It is not my place, but…Miss Clarissa is a most cherished friend. I fear for her as much as your mother, sometimes. She works tirelessly, running this household and taking care of the duchess. Everyone goes to her to solve their problems. Miss Clarissa handles everything with strength and grace, of course. I don't need a medical degree to see that it has taken its toll on her. I was alarmed to see her in such a state earlier, to learn she was shot. Your Grace, I have to ask, how did that happen?"

David sighed. He had a feeling he would be relaying this story many times in the near future and proceeded once again, to explain the circumstances from the previous day's debacle.

"How horrible, for both of you! You are most fortunate to be alive. You don't know who these men were? Why they would they accost your carriage? Was it mere robbery?"

"I'm not certain. The third man, the one Clarissa shot, said something about being glad his cohorts were gone, so he wouldn't have to split his reward."

"Reward? Do you believe they were hired to

kill you?"

"I'm not sure. I don't know what benefit it would be to anyone if Clarissa or I were dead."

"You are the Duke, and with the title come riches and power, or so I assume. Who would benefit by your demise?" Reginald queried. David frowned.

"I have no heir. I think if something would happen to me it would revert to my great uncle, Lord Grey. He was my Grandfather's half-brother, born the same year as my father, as I recall. I've never met the man. He lives far from here, at the family estate near Scotland, and to my knowledge has not shown any interest in the Dukedom."

"Perhaps you should have this matter investigated formally, if you do not feel the carriage incident was a random act. I do have a former school chum, a Detective Percival Darwin, who is with the Metropolitan Police in London. I would be happy to write to him on your behalf," the doctor offered. David raised his brows in surprise, and then nodded.

"Please do. We have not much in the line of law in Brookshire. His assistance would be much appreciated."

"Certainly, My Lord, I will get off a missive this very evening," the doctor said, then hesitated, as if unsure whether to continue. Finally, he spoke. "I worry, if someone wants to hurt you, if Miss Clarissa is safe here."

"I assure you; I can and will protect Clary with my life. She is...she is most important, to me." David said. He looked into the fire, but he could tell that Reginald was giving him an assessing look."

"Miss Clarissa is also important to me. I know she has no family."

"She has a family; we are her family!" David declared.

"I meant no disrespect. I understand she grew up here and you and the Duchess are close to her. But, I want to let you know, I do plan to offer for her hand. I know at this time she is overwhelmed with your mother's care, so I have not pressed my suit. However, that will not always be the case."

David felt something in his heart freeze, his fists clenched. "What makes you think that she would have you?" he asked.

"We have much in common. She is kind and learned. I feel she deserves more than to spend her whole life as a servant in someone else's home. She should have a home of her own, a husband and children. I believe we would be well suited to each other," the doctor stated.

David wished that there was something he could refute in that statement, but everything the man said was true. Clarissa was the daughter of a ladies' maid and a footman; she had been born into servitude. But she deserved more. She was refined and intelligent, beautiful and generous. She deserved so much more than the life she was born into. If he was truly a noble man, David would give Reginald his blessing, to court her. He was not so noble, however.

"I do not wish to stand in the way of Clarissa's happiness. However, I am not convinced that her happiness lies with you. If she should decide, of her own volition, that she wants to be with you, I would not stand in her way," he conceded.

"I suppose that is all I can hope for, for now." The doctor, stood up, and David stood too. "Your Grace, I must be going. I will get that missive off to Darwin tonight. I'll be back tomorrow, to check on my patients. Please have someone look in on Miss Clarissa every few hours. I have left an additional powder for her with the night nurse, if needed. If she spikes a fever or is in great pain, please, send for me immediately."

"Thank you, Doctor Bishop." David said formally, shrouding his conflicting emotions. He walked the man to the door of the library, where the butler was waiting in the hallway "This conversation has been...most enlightening. Franklin will show you out."

Reginald took his leave and David returned to his chair by the fire. Staring at the flames, he went over the conversation in his head. The doctor had essentially put him on notice. He wanted Clarissa. David should have been more prepared. He was sure that other men had taken an interest in her, over the years. If he were honest with himself, one of the reasons he avoided his mother's letters was that he never wanted to hear that Clarissa was courting, or engaged. She could do worse than Reginald Bishop. To be a doctor's wife was quite a coup for someone of her station. He should be happy that someone was willing to have her.

Once his mother was gone, her position as ladies' maid and companion would be unnecessary. He made Clarissa a promise, when Annabelle died so many years ago, that she would always have a home here, and he had meant it. He still meant it. But he recognized it was her choice, where she made her home. He just wanted her to choose to be with him always.

The butler cleared his throat, and David, startled. He hadn't even heard the man come back into the library. "Your Grace, the cook has prepared a light supper for you. We will serve at your convenience." Franklin told him.

"Thank you Franklin, I'll come to the dining room shortly," he acknowledged.

If Clarissa were awake, he would have asked her to dine with him. Setting down his brandy glass, he sighed. In the past he always dined with his mother, and when he was younger, Annabelle and Clarissa had always rounded out their evening dinners. Dinners filled with talk and laughter. Annabelle, whom he had adored like a beloved aunt, was gone, and soon enough his mother would be, too. How much longer would Clarissa stay after that?

Even in these last months in London, and estranged, he was comforted knowing that he had a family to go home to. Soon enough, he wouldn't have that. They would all be gone. The thought brought a lump to his throat and he blinked away the moisture that brightened his eyes. Straightening, he braced himself. Best to get use to solitary meals now, no doubt, he had many to look forward to in his future.

Chapter Nine

Clarissa awoke to a darkened room, the only light from the fireplace, whose embers were burned down to a faint orange glow. A few feet from her bed, she saw him. Much like the night before he was slumped to the side in a rocking chair, sound asleep. She moved her head experimentally. There was still some pain, but not nearly as bad as it had been. She felt somewhat recovered from the long carriage ride home. Her wound throbbed but she was sure in time that would go away. At the moment she had a much more pressing demand. She needed to use the chamber pot, badly. She pulled herself up and tried to stand up. She nearly toppled over, feeling woozy. Before she could hit the floor she felt strong arms come around her.

"Aye there Clary girl, where do you think you're going?"

"Davey?"

"Oh, I'm Davey again? I must say, I much prefer the reception I get from you when you're sick and weak." He said, helping her sit down on the edge of the bed. "Now, why are you trying to get out of bed?"

"I need to use the chamber pot," she admitted, embarrassed.

"Oh, I see. Would you like me to get one of the maids to help you?"

"No, please don't wake anyone. I can do this. Just leave me for a few minutes, please."

"Here, let me help you stand and once I'm sure you're steady, I'll step out. I'll just be right outside the door."

"You don't have to stay around. You should go to bed."

"For my own piece of mind, I'll wait until you're back in bed before I go anywhere. Here, now up we go." He helped her stand and let her lean on him as he led her to the foot of the bed. He edged the chamber pot out from under the bed, and set the lid aside.

She hung on to bed post with a shaking death grip and he seemed to question the wisdom of leaving the room at all. "Mayhaps I should just remain here. I promise I won't look."

"Get out!" she hissed. "I can't do this with you in the room."

He nodded grimly. "I'll be right outside the door," he promised. She nodded and as soon as he stepped around the threshold she squatted and relieved herself. By the time she was finished, she was shaking all over she barely had the energy to put the lid back on the chamber pot. She felt ready to collapse.

"Davey..." she whimpered. In a flash he was there beside her. Picking her up in his arms and depositing her back onto the mattress.

"Would you like some water?" he asked. She nodded and he poured her some from a pitcher on the bedside table. He held the cup to her lips as she sipped her fill. Finally, she pulled her head back and let him know she'd had enough. She lay back against the pillow. And he resumed his seat in the rocking chair, although he pulled it closer to the bed.

"Are you in pain? I have more of that powder from the doctor," he offered. She grimaced and shuddered, then shook her head no, as she turned to her side, facing him. Without thought, he reached out and took her hand.

"You should go to bed," she told him.

"I was in bed. I couldn't sleep, thinking about you in here all alone, and not well. So I came here, 'tis easier to sleep where I can open my eyes and see that you are safe."

"I am sorry for all the trouble I've caused. I know we should have waited to travel; I didn't imagine I would react to the carriage ride so poorly."

"I knew better. I should have listened to my instincts and not let my upset with you get in the way of what I knew was best."

"So it seems we both have much to be sorry for," she smiled sadly.

"I don't know that there are enough words to tell you of all of my regrets, my dearest Clary," he told her sincerely. "I am most sorry I left you here to bear the burden of my mother's illness and the running of the estate alone. I was selfish and angry, and acted like a spoiled child."

"You did," she agreed, and he had to laugh. She would never let him get away with anything. "But, you are here now. When I asked you to come, you came. And that is what matters."

"I'm not leaving, again," he promised her. "I am here to take my place as Duke, to run the estate as I should."

"I am glad to hear that. I will help anyway that I can."

"You've done more than enough. Surely you don't wish to spend your life as servant to this house."

Her brow furrowed. "This is my home. Where else would I want to be?"

"I think the fine doctor has designs on you. It is an offer to consider," he told her truthfully.

Her eyes widened in surprise. "Does he? Did he tell you this?"

"Yes, he did."

"Hmmmm."

"Really, that's all you have to say? Just

Hmmm?"

"Well what would you like me to say?"

"Do you want to be with him? Do you want to leave Hollister?"

"Wellll....he is rather handsome," she said thoughtfully

"I wouldn't know," was his dry response.

"Oh he is. All the ladies in the village are quite taken with him. When he first came to town I think every female within twenty miles came down with all manner of mild ailments just to get his attention."

"I can only imagine."

"He is quite nice to talk to. He's read all the works of Shakespeare and can quote nearly all the sonnets by heart. And he likes to carve little animals out of bits of wood. He made me a perfect carving of a cat, small enough to fit in the palm of my hand."

"Smart, and crafty, Lovely," David responded between gritted teeth.

"I wonder if he kisses well? Maybe I should give it a go and try him out. It would be awful to marry a man only to find out that he kisses like a wet toad," she said cheekily.

"A wet toad? And how would you know if he is a good kisser? What basis of comparison do you have?" he demanded to know.

"Well, to be honest, the only one I've ever kissed...is you," she said, sounding quite vulnerable all of the sudden. "And your kisses were the most perfect...I don't know how he could even compare. I'm not sure I care to find out, actually."

"That was so many years ago. No lips have touched yours since mine?" he asked in incredulous wonder. She shrugged.

"I've wanted no other."

"I...I don't know what to say."

"Reginald is a kind man, a good man. But he is not you," she told him simply. He felt humbled.

"I want so much...you know; I can never offer for your hand."

"I know. I remember that lecture from your mother, well. It is your duty to marry a title. It's the way of things," she sighed sadly.

"I wish...I wish we could walk away from all of this. Go somewhere, anywhere and start over with no expectations, where no one cares of titles and hierarchy."

"I would not want you to give up everything for me. No good could come of running away. You have a duty."

"A duty I was born into. I cannot help but resent that I have never been given the choice to choose my own path, to be a blacksmith or a merchant, or a doctor like your Mr. Bishop. No, I was born a Duke so a Duke, I must be," he said bitterly.

"You complain that fortune has smiled on you, when there are many who would take your place in an instant. I think you will make an admirable

Duke; I've always thought so. You are a leader of people, a natural caretaker, and a man of great intelligence. I think those qualities make you an ideal Duke."

"You flatter me. At least you see that I have qualities. The ladies of the ton see the title and nothing else."

"Have you...have you an eye on a future Duchess?"

"No one I have met can compare...I don't think I will ever find anyone to take as a Duchess."

"You must have an heir, but there is no hurry. Maybe next season you will go to London and find the one..."

"Clary...I found the one, the day I was born," he whispered.

"We shouldn't talk of this. You know, it cannot be."

"I know...it does not make it any less true."

"I...if I leave...if I marry Reginald, you'll be free of me. Maybe then it will be easier for you to find a proper Duchess," she suggested.

"If you truly felt you would be happy with him; I would not stand in your way. But do not do this for me; sacrifice your happiness for mine. I will not accept that."

"As you wish," she conceded. "I think...I am ready to go back to sleep now, I'm sure I'll be fine the rest of the night. You may go back to your bed, Your Grace," she told him.

"Ahhh...and like that, she is gone." He sighed sadly, standing up. "I will see you tomorrow, Clarissa. Sleep well." He left the room, closing her door behind him.

Chapter Ten

Clarissa watched the door clicked shut behind David. She'd lied about being sleepy. After sleeping all afternoon and evening she was now wide awake, and did not care to take any more of the elixir that Reginald had left behind. Still, she feared if she had spent another minute in David's presence she would have said or done something she regretted. As it was, the conversation had revealed that David was not as immune to her now, as she had once assumed. She tried not to let the thought give her hope. How many times had she let herself believe that they had a future, only to see him leave time and again?

Not once had he asked that she come with him.

She turned to her back and huffed out a sigh, staring into the dark at the ceiling. She did the right thing, retrieving him from London. It was well past time that he come home and takes his proper place. She thought of what he had said, about not wanting to be a Duke, and a niggle of guilt ate away at her conscious. If he knew the truth, what would he do? Would he walk away, yet again, this time never to come back?

She thought back to the fateful day, when she had overheard the truth. She had spent every waking moment at her mother's bedside, as had the duchess. She had known all her life that her mother was more than a mere servant to the duchess. They were the best of friends. When they had both lost their husbands in the carriage robbery, before she or David was born, that had solidified their bond in a way nothing else could have. They had banded together to make the best of a horrible situation, and both become stronger woman for it. Still, she had not understood the length that they had gone to, to protect their husband's legacies, until that day.

Annabelle's breathing had started to become labored. Clarissa had kept up a bright patter of conversation as she sat by her mother's bedside. "David should be here soon." She'd said. "He wrote he'd be here today by late afternoon. Won't it be good to see him, Mama?" She had said. Annabelle had turned her dimming brown eyes towards her, and it seemed that at David's name a bit of life had crept back into her face.

"My David," Annabelle, had said, taking a shuddering breath.

The duchess had been sitting on the other side of the bed. "Clarissa, may I speak to your mother alone?" She had said, although spoken gently, the words were no less a demand.

Clarissa had been privy to any number of private conversations between her mother and the duchess and could not understand what they could have to talk about that she would not be allowed to hear. Still, she did not argue but had risen and left the room, pulling the door closed behind her, however she had not latched it. Without remorse, she had stood on the other side, with her ear to the crack she had left open.

"Annabelle, David will be here soon," the Duchess said. "I leave it to you, if you wish to tell him the truth, I will not stop you."

"No...we promised each other...to the grave." Annabelle's gasping voice had said.

"What did we know in that moment when we made this promise? Newborn babes in our arms, we had no idea of the people they would become, how much we would love them. You have been the best mother to my dear Clarissa."

"And you, to my David. You will protect him with your life?"

"I would protect both of them with my life. As I always have, as you have too. I have not forgotten when you hid with my Clarissa, protecting her over your own child that day Lord Grey..."

"Lord Grey...may he be damned for what he did to our husbands," Annabelle all but spat. "I also will never forget how you protected my David, in that instance. Leaping from your bed, having just given birth and taking that poker to Lord Grey as he meant to kill my son."

Clarissa had not understood the conversation until she had heard Annabelle utter those words. Her son, David was Annabelle's son. That meant it had to mean...her mother was the duchess. She gasped out loud, and her hand had flown to her mouth.

It had been that moment when David had shown up.

"Clary," he had said from behind her, catching her unawares. She had spun around. Had he overheard too? But his eyes had been merely curious, at seeing her listening at the door, and maybe a bit sad. He knew of Annabelle's condition and would of course assume how difficult it would be for her, knowing her mother was near death.

He had grown a few inches while at school, and his shoulders had broadened. He looked not like a duke, but a young prince, to her, and not at all the boy she had spent her childhood, running hand in hand through the gardens and woods, with. For a moment she stared at him, wide eyed, because for the first time, she saw him as the man he would be, not the boy he had always been with her. Then he opened his arms, and she knew...she knew he was still David. Her David, she'd flown into his embrace.

She didn't know how long she had been in

his arms. She had spent weeks at her mother's bedside, worried, terrified, and despite a whole household full of people, and the duchess's assurances she had felt very much alone, until that moment.

When the door opened, they stepped apart. "David," the duchess had said. Would you like to see Annabelle?" she asked, and it was brought back to mind that David did not know...had no way of knowing that Annabelle was not merely a beloved servant to him and his mother, but his mother.

She wanted to tell him, had even opened her mouth to blurt out the truth to him, but then the realization that if he knew, everything between them would change. She glanced towards the duchess and saw her with new eyes.

This woman had given birth to her, yet she felt as if she were a stranger. Her mother, the mother who had rocked her to sleep, and mopped her tears and shown her unconditional love in every way, was Annabelle.

In her heart, she knew, no matter what, that fact would never change, and she did not want it to. She was proud to be Annabelle's daughter, and refused to think of herself as anything other than that. But David...his whole identity was built around being the Duke. With her, he would always be Davey, her companion and playmate. But to the world, as the Duke of Hollister, he would be an important man. His name would be recorded in history books, and he would govern and make important decisions. People's lives would rest in his hands, and she had no doubt that he would live up to that responsibility.

Who was she to take that away from him? She couldn't, and knew in that instance, despite everything, she would never reveal the truth to him. She knew enough of Annabelle and the duchess, to know that the decision to switch their children had cost them both, and that it was not a decision that had been easy for either of them. She would not throw away her mothers' sacrifice, neither of them.

It had been a few days later that Annabelle had died. She had been holding one of her mother's hands, and the duchess had held the other. David had been standing stoically at the end of the bed, tears in his eyes, as Annabelle had rattled off her last breath into silence.

The days following had been a blur. Annabelle was buried next to her husband in the cemetery next to the church. The Duchess tried to talk to her several times, but she had no wanted to listen. Finding out the secret of her birth seemed immaterial in the wake of the Annabelle's death. "You'll stay on, of course, as my companion and maid, just as your mother before you." The Duchess told her, and Clarissa stoically nodded her head. She had no feeling on the subject, she felt numb, and alone.

Only with David did she give in to the overwhelming grief that consumed her. Over the next week, every day, David would take her by the hand and they would make their way to the woods, to the oak tree that held the treehouse they had built as children after reading Robinson Crusoe and Swiss Family Robinson.

They'd climb the rope ladder and alone, with only David there for comfort, she would give in to her overwhelming grief and let the tears flow. He would hold her, his arms solid around her, keeping her from sliding into total despair.

It was then she began to realize that he was more to her than her friend and childhood companion. That she loved him, completely. In his arms she found comfort, but she also had begun to feel other things, want other things.

She thought of the night he had come to her room. She was certain he had not intended for things to go as far as they did. He had only wanted to comfort her, to be comforted by her in turn. But when his lips touched hers...

She let a tear slide from her cheek and absorb into the pillow. She had thought that night would be their beginning, but the sad reality was that it had been their end. Still, she remembered vividly what it had been like to be his, even if only for a few hours. She didn't know how she was going to get through the next weeks with David in such close proximity. Could she resist the need to be near him? Keep him at a distance, and keep the secret that had been their mother's burden, and now hers for the rest of her life?

She wasn't sure how she would, but as always in her life, she had no choice.

Chapter Eleven

David went to his own room and readied for bed. He tried not to think about what it was like the night before, to fall gently asleep with Clarissa's body snug beside him, climbing into a cold bed, alone held no appeal. Would he spend the rest of his life in this mire of conflict? Wanting the one person he could not have? He had told Clarissa that he was ready to take over his duties for the Duchy and he had been serious. He only wished that circumstances were different and that society would accept her as his duchess.

He remembered, in vivid detail, the morning that his mother had discovered them, curled in each other's arms in Clarissa's bed. It was shortly after Annabelle had died. They were mere youths of sixteen. She had been an innocent; he had been with a woman, a courtesan, just weeks earlier.

His friend's father, Viscount Fairchild, had taken him and his friend Kenton, to a high class brothel, and told them to take their pick. Her name had been Belinda, and he remembered how the Viscount Fairchild, had been so proud to be introducing him, the Duke of Hollister, to the lady. "Show him what it's like to be a man." He told her. "Teach him well." And she had.

He knew she was a bit older than he, but she was sweet, and patient, and put him at ease. She had been very thorough at explaining the bits and parts of a woman's body to him. Showing him how and where to touch, and what felt good. She showed him the spot at the apex of the slit that a woman's pleasure was to be found there. She explained quite seriously, that he should always remember to see to a woman's pleasure first, and not just rut away like a boar. He had taken her words to heart.

At Easter time, he found himself back at the estate. Annabelle had taken ill and he'd been summoned, by his mother. The following days were the saddest of his life as he dealt with his distraught mother and a sadly grieving Clarissa, not to mention his own very real grief.

Annabelle had been more than a servant to all of them.

She had been like a beloved aunt to him, someone to whom he could share his thoughts and confidences, without reprisal. He had been home for a few weeks, and knew he had to get back to Eton or risk losing his status at school. Still, he was quite reluctant to leave his mother and Clarissa alone in their mourning.

That night, he had heard Clarissa crying, when he walked by her room. He did not hesitate, but went inside, with only thought to comfort her. He climbed into bed with her, the way they had as children, during the storms and held her in his arms. As her tears quieted, the air around them changed. All he wanted to do was make her happy.

The emotions inside of him were overwhelming. Gently, he kissed her forehead, and she sighed. He kissed her closed eyes, and her cheeks, the corner of her mouth. Finally, he kissed her lips, and he felt as if the world had cracked open, and all the riches had rained down on him. She opened her mouth and without hesitation he delved his tongue inside. She wrapped her arms around him and returned his ardor, kiss for kiss, stroking his back, running her delicate hands through his hair.

Thoughts of what he had learned in Belinda's bed stirred him. Dared he? He promised himself he would stop at the first indication...he pulled her chemise up to her knees, to her thighs. She did not stop him. She reached for him and began to unbutton his shirt. He shrugged out of it. He untied the bow at the top of her chemise, and lowered the bodice. Her breasts were slight but perfect, tipped with tight rosy nipples. He took one in his mouth, and suckled and she arched into him, he stroked the other nipple. Belinda had told him how women liked that. It was very evident that her advice was right.

He raised her chemise up past her hips, she wore no undergarments and she was bare to him, except for a pale blond patch of hair that hid her most precious treasure. He touched her there and she froze for a moment, and then sweetly, parted her legs. "Trust me," he said and she cupped his face in her hands, and smiled at him, her eyes alight with desire. "I do," she said. In that moment he knew that he loved her, had always loved her. He could slay dragons for her, if need be. He touched her then, in that spot that Belinda had shown him, stroking her, feeling her become wetter and wetter, and her breath caught in pants. It was evident that she had never experienced anything like it and he felt overwhelmed that he could do this to her, for her. She clung to his shoulders. "What's happening?" she whispered desperately, fearing the sensations that were overwhelming her.

"Let go, my love, let it take you," he told her and she relaxed a bit and he knew the moment when pleasure took her, she quaked in his arms and he felt her spasm and clench at his fingers. She cried out her pleasure and he felt, all powerful, and desperate now to be inside her. She was still clinging to him, as he rushed to unbutton the fall of his britches. He had desperately wanted to breach her, but with the last bit of rationality he possessed, he did not. He did take Clarissa's hand and directed it to his member, and showed her the way to stroke it just right. Her small hand had a surprisingly strong grip and after a bit of hesitation, and his groaning encouragement, she managed to bring him to completion, his essence, like cream, against the skin of her belly in the moonlight.

"I love you, Clary," he'd said, "Forever." He'd sworn, tenderly enfolding her in his embrace. She sighed against his chest and he could feel her smile, and feel a tear fall against his skin.

"I love you, too, Davey. Forever," she murmured. He knew that nothing in his life would ever compare to the feeling of peace that her words gave him. They fell asleep in each other's arms, naked but for the sheet covering them.

The next morning, they both crashed into wakefulness as the Duchess stormed into the room. The next several moments had been chaos, as Drusilla screamed at the both of them in horror at what she was seeing. She made them both dress then took them each by an arm to the library, where she sat them down. It was evident her fury had in no way abated, and had to step away and take several deep breaths before she calmed enough to look at both of them. He had stared defiantly back. Clarissa was cowering, with her head down. She didn't look at him, just cried softly.

"Mother...I will marry her. I want to marry her," he said, his voice cracking. Drusilla turned on him.

"You most certainly will not marry her, or touch her ever again! You are a Duke; you were raised to marry a title. That is your most important responsibility. You had no business doing... Clarissa is...the daughter of a servant. She is not for you. She will never be for you. It is just not done," she said, her voice taking on an erringly strident tone.

"As Duke, I can marry whom I wish. I love her," he asserted.

"What can you know of love? You are a child. She..." she said, pointing at Clarissa, "is still a child. I am so angry at you both! So ashamed of your behavior, I don't have words!" She said turning her back on them both, visibly shaking, her arms crossed.

"You seem to have plenty of words," he retorted, sarcastically. She turned around then and stepped towards him and slapped him hard across the face. Behind him, he heard Clarissa gasp, and choked back a sob. For a moment he kept his head turned to the side, stunned. He had perhaps gone too far, but to cower now would be unthinkable. He turned his face back to his mother and stared back defiantly.

"You have no idea what you've done!" she cried. "Clarissa is our charge. You defile her; in her own bed...I am only glad Annabelle is not here to see this." She turned away in disgust. Clarissa broke down sobbing, and he wanted to go to her, but his mother stepped in front of him, blocking his way.

"Go to your room. Now, I need to speak to Clarissa, alone. I will be up to speak to you shortly." He hated leaving his mother alone with Clarissa, but seeing as there was no dissuading her, he left, slamming the library door behind him.

He went to his room and waited. He would just make her see reason. He loved Clarissa, she was meant to be his. He had always known it. The moments in her arms the night before, only cemented that. It had all been so sweetly beautiful, until his mother had walked in and shattered it all. If his mother refused to let him marry her, they would run away, to Scotland and get married at Gretna Green. Maybe they'd go to America, he had read much about the colonies and the land that was opening up further inland that was fertile and ready to be tamed. They could get a bit of land to call their own and start a family. He had never so much as planted a flower before, but he was strong and smart and he could learn...

His mother knocked on the door, and let herself in without waiting for a response. He glared at her sourly. She met his glare with one of her own. She crossed her arms in front of her and then quietly began to speak "I...I am sorry I struck you. I was wrong to do that," she said.

He refused to acknowledge her apology, and kept his glare firm on her face.

With a frustrated sigh, she sat down, in a chair facing him, and leaned forward. "I know you have feelings for Clarissa. She is a lovely girl, with many wonderful qualities. I cannot fault you for that. But...she is not for you. Never mind the fact that you are both much too young to be considering marriage, you cannot consider this girl. There are certain...expectations of a Duke, first and foremost is that he must marry someone befitting his title. Annabelle was my dearest friend, and I promised her to take care of her child. In the event that you did marry Clarissa, you would be setting her up for a world of misery. She is not of the ton. She would never be accepted as a peer."

"Married to a Duke, she would have to be accepted," he reasoned. She shook her head, sat down next to him, and took his hand in hers.

"Please, listen to me and hear what I'm saying. You do not know this world. Your exposure has been limited. The ladies in the peerage are brought up to know how to cut a person with a word, or the turn of a cheek. There are many ways they can make a person feel...unvalued no matter what title they've been given. I do not want that for Clarissa."

"These women who would look down on her, these are the sorts of woman you would have me choose from, to marry, instead?"

"It is what you must do."

"I will give it up, then. I don't need to be Duke; I just want to be with her."

"You can't mean that! You have no idea the sacrifices I have made to secure this legacy! I will not let you throw this away," she said angrily. "If you walked away you would have nothing. No money, no land. Your power would be gone. The estate would go to ruin."

"But…I would have her."

"But nothing to offer her, you have a greater responsibility to more than just yourself. Many lives will depend on you living up to your responsibilities, Clarissa's included," she said, quietly. He wanted to deny her words, but she was right. If he was Duke, the peerage would never accept Clarissa as his duchess. If he ran away with her, he would have nothing at all to offer her. Either scenario led to Clarissa's unhappiness. He was well aware of the legacy he was born into. A position he did not want, nor ask for, but was obliged to fulfill. The only way he could ever protect Clarissa, and the people of his district, was to take his rightful place as Duke. Defeated, he slumped down, his head in his hands. His mother put her arm around him. "I feel I am to blame for this. I knew you two were close. I had no idea you were so…I should have foreseen this. I…think it best that I send Clarissa away. I have friends in France…" She said. He jumped up and whirled to face her.

"No! This is her home. I will leave, if one of us must go. Promise me Mother, she will always have a home here," he said adamantly.

"I…yes, I promise."

"I ask one other thing, please, do not shame her for this. I went to her. The fault lies only with me. You must never mention this incident again, to her." He was fervent, in this. She gave him a sad, assessing look that was almost respected.

"I can agree to that."

"Then I will leave tomorrow, and go back to Eton." He stated. She nodded jerkily.

"David…I am most sorry. I know you are unhappy about this, and Clarissa is, too. But it is for the best."

"Pardon me, if I do not take your word for it Mother." He said coldly. She sighed in resignation, and left him then.

He had tried to find Clarissa, to talk to her, but his mother had taken great pains not to leave them alone together. A footman had even been posted in the hallway outside of Clarissa's bedroom. After being thwarted at every turn, he went to bed that night feeling nothing but anger and despair.

The next morning, he had the servants pack his

bags, as he went in search of Clarissa. This time, he would have his say, he insisted to himself. Surprisingly, he found her alone, in the breakfast room. "Clary...I am leaving," he said. She looked up and he saw the last bit of hope die in her eyes. But she stiffened her spine and nodded.

"Safe travels...Your Grace," she said, casting her eyes down. It was then he knew he had completely lost her. They had never stood on ceremony, and had always addressed each other familiarly. Now, she acted in her position as a servant in his household and the deferential tone she took, broke his heart. He did not give into it until he was alone in the carriage, taking him to London. In silence he had grieved for the life he could never have with the one person he loved over all else.

Returning to school, he wrote to Clarissa many times, but after months with no answers to his letters, he simply gave up, and gave into the silence between them. He had come back to the estate periodically, over the years, but would only stay for a few days. Clarissa would treat him with polite deference, and, inevitably, he and his mother would exchange words in anger and he would feel compelled to leave, again. Much of his dealings with his mother went through their man of business. He attended university, but only barely kept up with his studies. After university he moved to London where he lived the life of many of the young nobles. Gambling and drinking to excess. He sought company with courtesans, but their attention left him feeling more sad than satisfied.

On the rare occasion that the Duchess came to London, with Clarissa, he made a point of staying out of their way. The young ladies of the ton had let him know, in no uncertain terms, that they would all love to be the future Duchess of Hollister. He compared each to Clarissa and found them all lacking. He knew someday he was obligated to marry, and provide an heir. He expected someday, he'd meet some well-bred lady who was tolerable and do his duty, but he did not foresee that happening anytime soon, if ever. Now, he was back, sharing the same walls as Clarissa and he were not sure how he would be able to bear being in her presence, and not touch her, not hold her. A lifetime of her deference sounded like purgatory. Maybe it was what he deserved. On that sad thought, he drifted off to sleep.

Chapter Twelve

The door to the Duchess Drusilla's bedchamber stood ajar. Clarissa knocked, and announced herself before walking in. Drusilla sat up in bed, a breakfast tray piled high with food sat in front of her. She looked quite pale, but her eyes were bright, and she smiled on seeing Clarissa's face. "Oh Clarissa dearest, I am happy to see you up and about. I was so worried yesterday when I saw you. Are you feeling much better?"

"I am, I still have a bit of a sore head, but the dizziness and nausea seems to be gone now. What of you? I feel I must reprimand you for getting out of bed, yesterday. You know you aren't strong enough to be running about the manor," Clarissa chastised lovingly. The Duchess brushed aside her concern with, with an impolite gesture and Clarissa had to laugh.

"I had to see for myself that you were alright. When Betty came in and told me that she had seen you sicken outside and that David had to carry you to your room...well I imagined the worst. I am still not entirely certain what happened."

"Just as David said last night, our carriage was accosted by highwaymen, and one of them took a shot at the carriage and apparently I did not duck low enough. It just grazed the crown of my head, I expect that I will only have to wear this plaster for a few more days, which is not a very good thing as it clashes with all my dresses," she said, making light of her injury. The Duchess's expression told her she didn't buy her breezy story for a minute, but would let it go.

"These highwaymen, did you recognize any of them?"

"No...not at all. I assume they intended to rob us. Why else would they have stopped us?"

"I am worried that Lord Grey is up to his old tricks. I am still not entirely convinced he wasn't behind the incident that happened to Dorian and George so many years ago. And before that, Dorian's older brother also died under mysterious circumstances. Nothing could ever be proven, but this incident has his stink all over it."

"It's been so many years. Why would he wait until now to try anything? Do you really think he's behind this and David is in real danger?"

"I have no evidence, I never have, which is why he has been a free man for over twenty-five years. It's just a feeling. I have controlled Lord Grey for years, he is under restraint not to come near

David or I, or forfeit being cut off from his only source of income. But I fear he has found out of my poor health and with David coming into the full entailment soon, on his twenty fifth birthday, he may see this as his one chance to take over the dukedom."

"You need to tell David this. Your Grace...you need to tell him everything, the whole truth."

"Clarissa, my darling girl, what do you think David would do? Annabelle and I explained to you years ago, why it had to be this way. What it would mean if anyone found out."

"Last night...David and I spoke. I know you feel this is the right thing to do, but it is a burden to him. He does not care for the title. If he knew how he was being used..."

"This is why we mustn't tell him. Soon, this will all be his, and I have made sure that provisions are in place for you. Lord Grey is an evil man and I will not let him take what is rightfully mine to pass along."

"It is tiring, this lie. I know why it is necessary, but it is a heavy burden to bear. When we were young, we had no secrets between us. It is so difficult to know that with every word between us I am lying to him. I want him to be happy, and I don't think he is, or has been, in ages. I so wanted to tell him last night. But I knew he would feel betrayed."

"I know, darling. Believe me, I am well aware

of the feelings of guilt, holding something like this inside can cost. For years, Annabelle and I held the burden alone. It was her decision to tell you. She knew you could handle this, and would understand. But we both know David. He would not be so forgiving, to either of us. I don't know that we can afford to tell him."

"I will abide by your wishes, for now. But please know, if he discovers the truth, on his own, I cannot deny it, if he asks me. I won't lie to him."

"If he discovers the truth, there will be little use denying it. I can only hope he never does, for his own peace of mind." A knock came to the door, and Doctor Bishop's smiling face popped in.

"I see my two favorite patients are up. How are you ladies feeling today?" He asked, walking to the side of the bed. He pulled out his pocket watch and took Drusilla's wrist and checked her pulse.

"I am feeling a bit better this morning. I may have them take me out to the garden today." Drusilla told him.

"How is your pain?"

"Tolerable. I will leave it at that."

"I think you only tell me that because you do not want me to medicate you." He frowned. She gave him an exasperated look.

"Your powders only make me sleepy, the pain is being managed. I promise if it gets to be too much I will drink down one of your magic elixirs."

"See that you do." With that he turned his attention to Clarissa, "how about you, young lady? How is the head today?" He lifted the dressing at the crown of her head, then produced a salve from his bag and reapplied it to the wound, before redressing it.

"I feel much relieved. The wound is a bit tender, but the headache is almost gone and I'm not feeling the dizziness or nausea this morning."

"Excellent. I would still like you to rest as much as possible over the next few days. I have no doubt you will make a full recovery. Perhaps you could join the Duchess in the garden today. I think fresh air and sunshine will do you both good."

"Well, I feel in this case I would be happy to follow the Doctor's orders."

"See that you do," Reginald said, packing up his bag. "Ladies, I shall take my leave. If you should need me, for any reason, please send for me."

"Of course Doctor, I shall see you out," Clarissa said.

"No need. I know the way. Is the Duke up and about, do you know? I did want to have a word with him."

"He may be in the breakfast room. I thought I heard him going down the stairs while I was coming to see the Duchess."

"I will check there. Good day, ladies," he said,

bowing his head as he left the room. Clarissa turned back to the Duchess.

"I shall help you bathe and dress, and then have a few of the footmen come up and assist you down to the garden."

"Thank you, dearest. And then I would like to see David. Could you make sure the ledgers come out with us, when we go to the garden? I do feel like I should go over those with him, while I am still able."

"Surely, you do not need to do that today? You should just enjoy your time with David, and not bring estate business into it, at least for a few days," Clarissa admonished.

"My dear girl, at this time my life remaining is measured in hours and days, not months and years. It would be remiss of me not to make sure that David was up to the task of running this estate when I am gone. As it is, I wonder if I have done him an injustice over the years, by not insisting he take on more responsibilities earlier. I so wanted him to have his freewheeling days of early manhood, without the burden of all this hanging over him. I only hope I have not left it too late."

"I am sure that he will be able to muddle through just fine. And I will be here to help, I've done most of the book work over the last few months and I'm sure he will be able to take over with little problem."

"You are probably right. Still, it would ease my mind to know that he is well versed on all the facets of the entailment."

"We will both make sure he is up to speed," Clarissa assured her. "Now, finish your breakfast, Your Grace, while I ring for your bath."

Chapter Thirteen

David ambled through the portico to the garden beyond. His mother and Clarissa sat on wicker lounges under the shade of a tree, looking out over the rose garden. This garden was his mothers' pride and joy. She spent many hours tending her roses here during the warm months. During the winter she tended her roses in the solarium. As long as he lived, he was certain that every time he should come across the scent of a rose, he would think of his mother, just as he thought of Clarissa when he smelled lemon verbena. It was early spring yet, and few blooms where out. He sincerely hoped she would be able to see her garden, one last time while it was in full bloom.

"David, darling, I am so glad to see you up this morning." His mother said, smiling. Despite the warmth, she wore a heavy shawl around her and floppy hat on her head. Her face looked haggard; her cheek bones were sharp angles, but her eyes were alert and bright today, which reassured him. Beside her, Clarissa looked lovely in a soft pink floral day gown, and a cream colored shawl, her long golden hair braided and hanging over her shoulder. If it weren't for the plaster marring her scalp, she would have looked like the picture of health.

"Good morning, ladies. I am relieved to see you are both looking much better today."

"I do feel a bit chipper this morning, having you home is the best of tonics," the Duchess told him. "Come, sit with us, David. We have much to discuss." She said, indicating the adjoining wicker seat. He sat down, and looked over at Clarissa.

"Is the head better today?"

"Much, the doctor changed my dressing this morning, and seems to think I will be completely healed in no time. He said he wanted to speak to you before he left, did he find you?"

"Yes, he did. He advised me that he had sent a missive to a former schoolmate of his who is a police detective in London, regarding the attack on our coach."

"Does this mean you don't feel it was a random attack?" Clarissa asked.

"I cannot stop thinking about the words of the third man that he would not have to split his reward. This tells me someone was paying them to do that, but who?"

"I can tell you who. Lord Grey!" exclaimed the

Duchess.

"Why would he do that? I've never even met the man."

"He saw you one time, on the day you were born. He bullied his way into my room, shortly after I had given birth and was in a rage. I was terrified he would murder you in your cradle. I had to bash him with a poker to stop him. I fear this is history repeating itself. I am convinced he was behind the attack that led to the deaths of your fathers," the Duchess declared vehemently. "I have tried for years to keep him on a short leash, but he must be aware of my precarious health, and knowing that you come into the bulk of your inheritance on your next birthday...he may feel this is his opportunity to strike."

"Wait...mother, what happened the day I was born? I've never heard this before," he asked. He knew that he and Clarissa had been born on the same day, but very little else regarding the day of their mutual birth.

"I still don't even know how he knew I had given birth that day. Annabelle and I were in my bedchamber, with the two of you. We had both given birth within hours of each other, as you know. We were sleeping. We heard a ruckus. I ordered Annabelle into the wardrobe with Clarissa. He burst into the room and came at me, and knocked me down, then saw the crib where you lay, he pulled off your blanket and when he saw you were a male...he raised his fist. I was certain he intended to end you. I grabbed the poker and cracked his arm with it. By then, the staff was there and hauled him away. All these years I've controlled him; he only receives his monthly stipend from the estate if he stays more than fifty miles from you. Which means he is not allowed near the estate, and was not allowed near London while you were living there, either?"

"If he is being kept so far away, how would he know that you were ill, or know that I would be on the road that day?"

"I don't know. I hate to think that anyone from our staff has been keeping him abreast of our business. But I can't be surprised. He's always felt like he was the rightful heir, instead of Dorian, being the second son, and not the grandson of the Duke. I know he and Dorian were the same age and from what I understood he was always an angry bully. Dorian did his best to ignore him, but I fear that he underestimated Lord Grey's greed."

"We have no proof. All of the gunmen that came after us are dead. Maybe I should confront Lord Grey."

"No! Promise me, David. You won't go anywhere near that man!" the Duchess demanded.

"Your Grace, if he has gone to this much trouble to hurt you, hurt us, I doubt that anything good would come from facing him." Clarissa had to agree.

"So am I just to wait for him to strike again?"

"Perhaps this detective from London will be able to help." Clarissa reasoned. "It might be best if we add some extra footmen to watch the estate."

"I'm not sure that footmen could provide adequate guard. Are there any militia men living in the village?" David asked.

"There is Captain Lucas Welch, and his brother Lt Darius. They fought in Portugal, during the civil unrest there. They both sustained injuries and were released from service, but they are quite capable men. The brothers took over their older brother's farm, when he passed," Clarissa told him.

"Excellent. I'm sure they would be of assistance," the duchess agreed. "I've met the brothers, most impressive men, and highly intelligent, especially Lt Darius. He stops by Hollister House at least once a week to make use of our collection of books in the library, he and I and Clarissa have had some marvelous discussions on many subjects to mention. I had wanted to talk to you of their operation. They are forgoing the growing of wheat and hay to grow hops and barley. They have a large century's old cider house on their land that they converted into a beer distillery. I have had the chance to taste their brew and I must say it is quite marvelous. I feel with the proper backing they have a chance of great success."

"That is quite enterprising. Regardless of their help with the security situation, I would like to talk to them about that."

"I thought you might. Maybe you should have them summoned to the estate, and discuss this with them?"

"I'll do better than that. I will go see them. It's time I took a look around our lands and got to know the tenants. That would be a good place to start."

"That's an excellent idea. But do take a few men with you. After this incident I don't feel you can be too cautious."

"I will. Now I see you have the ledger books. Shall we go over those?"

"Yes. Clarissa knows more about the more recent details but there are a number of enterprises and tenants that work our land and I want to make sure that they are all taken care of properly."

"Yes Mother. I couldn't agree more. Let's get to it."

Chapter Fourteen

MacPherson jumped every time the door to the tavern opened. His eyes were still both blackened, but at least now the swelling has gone down a bit and he could see. It still hurt to breathe through his broken nose. The horse ride to the tavern in the next village was a jarring, painful event. If he had any sense, he would have ignored the summons, but he had learned long ago that Lord Grey was not one to be trifled with. Finally, the door opened and the man entered. The years had not been kind to Lord Grey. MacPherson remembered when he had first encountered him, as a ten-year-old boy, living on the streets of London. He had been caught breaking into Lord Grey's home, quite red handed with the loot stuffed into his pockets. He knew the penalty for thievery could range from banishment to death. Lord Grey had offered him an alternative. Come work for him. Be his spy, in return he would never face charges.

Lord Grey had instigated his finding employment in his nephew, Lord Dorian's household as a tiger and stable boy. MacPherson had taken instantly to his new job, and found he truly loved working with the horses. Lord Dorian had been very kind to him, and when he married the Duchess, she had also been a benevolent employer. On a monthly basis, he had met with Lord Grey and told him what was happening in the house. MacPherson hadn't been sure, then, why Lord Grey would need to know about such things like the trips the Duke planned or the Duchess being with child.

He'd been on the carriage the day that the Duke and George were accosted. He had actually told Lord Grey of the planned trip just the day before. Mac had been so excited to be included in the putting to buy more breeding stock for the stables. He'd sat atop the carriage next to George.

Like the Duchess, George's wife Annabelle was with child; George was ecstatic that he was going to become a father, as was the Duke. As an orphan, MacPherson could only imagine how lucky the babes would be to have such fine men for fathers. He liked to pretend George or the Duke was his father, or at least his older brother.

Suddenly the highwaymen were upon them, and the carriage lurched to a stop. George shouted at him to run, and so he had, to the edge of the woods. From his vantage point among the trees, he saw clearly what happened. George had tried to protect the Duke, but he'd been mortally wounded, and soon after, Duke Dorian also met his fate.

Lord Grey had then stepped out from an outcropping of rocks where he'd been hiding, and handed off payment to the highwaymen. He called MacPherson out. "I know you're there, little Mac. Come out where I can see you," he'd demanded. On shaking legs, MacPherson had obeyed.

"You'll not be telling anyone of this, now, will you boy." Mac had shaken his head fiercely, out of a state of self-preservation.

"Good lad. Just you remember that. If I swing, you swing right beside me. That I can promise you," he'd said, then laughed, laughed as blood still seeped out from the lifeless bodies of George and Duke Dorian as they lay in a tangled heap in the dirt. "Now, you'll be telling them what happened. That they were killed by highwaymen, but you won't be able to remember what they looked like, of course, because you ran, without getting a good look. And remember, you didn't see me. Like I said, if I swing, you swing beside me. Remember that." In a stuttering, stammering voice, MacPherson promised.

Hearing horses coming around the bend, Lord Grey took his leave and galloped away through the woods, leaving a terrified, heartbroken Mac behind.

His next moments were a blur, as a party of Samaritans stopped to assist him. He told them what happened but didn't dare mention Lord Grey, and gave only the vaguest description of the assailants.

His greater horror and shame came later, when he was presented to the Duchess and Annabelle. Both ladies were heavy with child. As he stuttered through the telling of the events to the widows, he stared at the floor, unable to meet their eyes, lest they see that his duplicity.

He'd shuffled back to his quarters, over the stable, to find a note from Lord Grey ordering him to alert him the minute the Duchess gave birth. He did as bid, his child's mind not seeing any way around it. Though he had not known of Lord Grey's plans to murder the Duke, and George, he felt responsible. He vowed to himself that no matter what, he'd watch over their children. That was the least he could do.

Over the years, Lord Grey still badgered him for information, which he gave reluctantly. He'd hated telling him of the estrangement between her and Duke David, or of the Duchess taking ill.

He would never have told Lord Grey at all, of the trip to London to retrieve David, except the man had wanted to meet him the very day he was leaving with Miss Clarissa. Why hadn't he realized that Lord Grey was still so capable of evil? Twenty-five years of virtually no activity from the man had left MacPherson complacent.

He shuddered to think that he had almost let his own son, sixteen-year-old Robbie, come along on the trip. Thank God he had decided to leave Robbie behind to care for a mare in the stable about to foal. His son had been by his side and often helped with the delivery of the foals since he was a wee lad, and Mac had felt secure leaving him in charge of the stable.

Aye, if Robbie had been there, if those men had laid a hand on him or pointed a gun at him...he should have known. Should have remembered... well he would not fall into that trap again. The Duchess and her son the Duke, and Miss Clarissa, he owed them his allegiance. Not to this man. Never again.

"Mac, you summoned me. I assume you have news to tell." Lord Grey said "I see you've had a bit of an altercation, man. I hope you're alright."

"You Bastard, you know you're responsible for the condition I'm in!"

"Mind your tongue! Remember who you are speaking to. I can't say I know what you're talking about. You've taken to brawling?"

"Your men did this to me, and tried to kill the Duke and Miss Clarissa!"

"Tried? So I take it they were unsuccessful... pity that." Lord Grey said

"As if you were not there! I'm here to tell you, I'm done. No more. I'll not be your slave any longer," MacPherson declared.

"Oh, but I think you will."

"I am going to the Duke and the Duchess; I don't care if I hang. I am telling them the truth."

"So you don't have a care any longer for your own neck; But what of your wife, Betty, is it? And you have a son too...I'm sure he's a smart boy, just like his father. I'm sure he would be more than happy to take your place."

"You'll not be touching my family! They have nothing to do with this!"

"But without you to protect them from unfortunate...accidents, how will they survive? Betty is still quite the lusty wench, isn't she? Maybe I should give her a go? I've always had a thing for widows. They're so needy and desperate to please."

"You fucking bastard! If you lay a hand on my wife..."

"Sit down you fool! You'll what? Kill me? Despite it all, I am still a noble man and you are but a stable hand. You don't think you would pay for that? You think your wife and son would ever be able to find employment after what you did? Leaving them to life as beggars on the street... surely you remember what that was like, Mac. You'd want no better for them?"

MacPherson tasted bitter defeat. What could he do, to confess that he had been in league with Lord Grey all this time, feeding him information?

That he had some involvement in the deaths of the former Duke and George, and had relayed information that had led to the carriage incident... he'd go to prison or worse. Who would take care of Betty and Robbie? And if Lord Grey succeeded and became the Duke...what then? It was a hellish path either way.

It was then that he decided he'd keep playing this game. But now, he would be the one making the rules. A bit of misdirection...ah yes. MacPherson nearly smiled, thinking how he could trap Lord Grey in his own web. However, he kept his expression solemn as he nodded.

"I'll do anything you say, My Lord. Just don't hurt my family."

"I'm glad to see that you have come to your senses. Now tell me, how is the Duchess' health?"

"Much better, it's been quite the miracle, these last few days. She seems quite her old self again."

"Really? I thought she was near dying."

"Not to see her today. She was up and about, tending to her garden. Maybe seeing her son again has put the spring back in her step."

"I see...hmmm."

"In fact His Grace was talking this morning that he might just go back to London, as he's not needed here."

"I'm sure you will keep me apprised of his return trip."

"Yes, My Lord. The moment he decides to be on

his way, I will let you know."

"Excellent." Lord Grey stood up. "I'll be on my way. So I will meet you a week from today, same time, unless I hear otherwise from you."

"Of course, My Lord, as always."

Lord Grey stood, and threw a few coins on the table before he strode out of the tavern, leaving MacPherson at the table.

MacPherson took a long drink of his ale and wiped his hand across his mouth, and thought about his life. He was not a man who lived in anger. He had a wife he loved and the adoration of a fine, strong son. He loved his work with the horses, and lived rent free in a cozy home over the stables with his family. Given his start in life as a beggar and thief, he was proud man he'd become.

He'd be damned if that bloody noble bastard was going to take that away from him. Now, he needed to make a plan to take him down, expose Lord Grey for the gutless bully he was and get rid of him for good.

Without losing his own head.

Chapter Fifteen

As they approached the Welch's farm, David reined his elderly horse in, deciding then and there that he was going to send a message to his friend, Viscount Kenton Fairchild, to have his own horse brought to him from London. There weren't many horses under saddle in their stables. He'd learned to ride on Osiris as a boy, and he was a steady mount, but now, old and slow. His usual mount at Hollister house, Persephone, had foaled the day before, and could not be ridden for some time. If he intended to stay, he wanted his favorite horse here.

Robbie MacPherson rode by his side. He'd been eager to go with David, and David was reminded of Robbie as a young boy, the way he had followed him and Clarissa around the estate. He was sixteen now, nearly a man, but still very much a boy.

David remembered now, when he was sixteen himself, when everything in his life had changed. He'd felt like a man then, but now, looking back, he realized that he, like Robbie, had been nothing but a boy wanting to be grown well before he was ready. Still, if he and Clarissa had had the chance...he caught himself before he could let his mind go down that road. What was done was done. He'd resolved that he would stop regretting the past and only look forward to the future.

On his left was Lawrence, a youngish footman who had only recently started working at the estate. Not much of a security detail, David thought, but at this time beggars couldn't be choosers. He sincerely hoped that the Welch Brothers might be of more help.

They could hear the sound of hammering and sawing, and followed the noise behind the house. From this vantage point David could see several acres showing rows furrowed soil with bits of green poking through.

The trio rounded the house and came into sight of two men. David assumed they had to be the Welch brothers. "Good afternoon, gentlemen," David called out.

The two men immediately stopped what they were doing and approached. David noted right away that both men were of an immense height, easily several inches over his own six-foot height, and nearly twice as broad. Shirts had been discarded and their bodies were lean, but thickly muscled. Both men had dark russet hair that hung past their shoulders, that seemed more red than brown in the bright sunlight, and brilliant teal blue eyes that stood out against their sun burnished skin.

One man had an eyepatch over his left eye and a scar that bisected his face on that side giving him a sinister air.

The other man had an eager, intelligent expression and as they approached, David noted he walked with a stiff legged limp that favored his right leg, but it did not seem to stop him from working up a sweat.

"May we help you?" the man with the eyepatch asked, coming towards them. His arms crossed over his massive chest.

"I'm David Thoroughgood, Duke of Hollister. I have a matter of some importance that I wish to discuss." David told them, as he dismounted. Robbie and Lawrence dismounted as well. The men exchanged a frowning look between them, and David at once wished his tone hadn't come off as quite so imperious.

"Welcome Your Grace, I am Lucas Welch, and this is my brother Darius Welch," the man with the eye-patch said, inclining his head "We've not made your acquaintance, before, though we have met your mother, the Duchess many times. These last several months, it has been Miss Clarissa that has come to call."

"Yes, so I've been told. I might have had her come with me to make introductions but unfortunately we were involved in an altercation, and she was injured, which is why I've come to enlist you gentleman. I understand that you both have military training."

"Miss Clarissa was hurt?" Darius asked, stepping forward in alarm. His brother held him back with an arm.

"Yes, My Lord, we served in the military, and are both combat trained. What happened to Miss Clarissa?"

"We were coming from London, by carriage, when we were accosted by highwaymen. We think that they were lying in wait for us, or at least, for me. We were attacked and Miss Clarissa was shot..."

"Shot!" Darius exclaimed. "Is she hurt badly? Dead?"

"She was grazed at the crown of her head. She's fine, or she will be. Although, even hurt she managed to take out one of the three men, and I took care of the other two. But, we have reason to believe that my great-uncle may behind this, although we have no proof. Until we can get proof, we need protection. I am hoping I can rely on you gentleman to provide that."

"Of course..." Darius answered, simultaneously Lucas replied

"No, we are no longer soldiers." Darius turned back on his brother, an incredulous expression on his face.

"Lucas, Miss Clarissa was shot, we can't refuse

them protection."

"Darius, must I remind you we have work here...important work. We need to get these bins finished before the crops are ready to harvest and the brewing equipment put together, not to mention the brewing room. There are not enough hours in the day as is...we simply do not have the time to do this."

"Might I offer a trade of services? I, and Robbie and Lawrence here, to help you a few hours a day, in exchange for your protection, as the situation warrants."

"Pardon me, my lord, but what do you know of physical labor?" Lucas scoffed. David lifted his chin and looked him directly in the eye.

"I'm strong, and I studied architecture at university. I feel that the building of storage bins is not beyond me." David asserted. Lucas gave him an assessing look, and David realized that he was not one to be impressed by titles or privilege.

David dispensed with his jacket and rolled up his sleeves. "Tell me what needs to be done. I am at your disposal." Following his lead, Robbie and Lawrence also rolled up their sleeves. Lucas did not hesitate to assign them each task and soon they were all at work, hammering boards to the frame making up the bins.

David found he actually relished swinging the hammer, something he hadn't done since he had been a boy, when MacPherson had helped him and Clarissa build a treehouse in the woods, after he'd read Swiss Family Robinson. He'd been immensely proud of that tree house, and it had been one of the reasons he had studied architecture at University. Those had been among the few classes he had enjoyed. He and Clarissa had spent many an hour in that treehouse, talking and pretending. He wondered, if it was still there? When he got back to the estate he would have to check.

It was well into the afternoon when Lucas called a halt. They had accomplished quite a lot in the hours that they had been there, finishing not one, but two of the tall storage bins. David felt he could easily have kept going but realized they were out of wood. He felt oddly disappointed.

While they had worked the men had devised a plan. Lucas and Darius would take turns patrolling the estate at night, and would also instruct all the males on the estate in weaponry and defense.

The Welches agreed to come back with him to Hollister House, and he would call a meeting of all of the men of the estate. Between Franklin, the butler, and the footmen and a few others who worked in the stable and the gardens he had eleven men, twelve counting himself. Surely that would be enough to curtail any threat made against them? With the work done on the bins, the Welch's accompanied him back to the estate.

He had sent Robbie and Lawrence ahead, to gather the men together at the stable yard. The assembled men all looked to him expectantly, as they arrived. For a moment he felt a bit out of his depth, realizing that he was indeed asking them all to put their lives on the line for him. He wanted no one hurt on his behalf. But then he thought of Clarissa, and stiffened his resolve. For her, he would do anything and he was certain that every one of these men present felt the same way; they all knew her, most since childhood.

He lifted his chin and looked them all in the eye, letting them know he was indeed the Duke, and they were there to serve his household.

"Gentlemen, I thank you for your time. As most of you know, there was an altercation on the road as Miss Clarissa, MacPherson and I were traveling here from London. We believe that this was not a random robbery, but an attempted assassination against me. Mac here bore most of the brunt of this attack," he said indicating MacPherson who still clearly showed the bruises about his face. "Miss Clarissa was also hurt, and nearly killed. I cannot allow that to happen again. I have enlisted Captain Lucas Welch and his brother Lt. Darius Welch to aid us in this endeavor," he said looking around at everyone present.

"All the men of this estate, including myself, are going to train with the Welch's, so that we may be able to defend Hollister House and all its inhabitants, in the event, whomever, was behind this attack, tries again. Men, do I have your agreement and cooperation?" He asked. To their credit every man gave his agreement. It seemed most of them even stood up straighter and David was heartened at their support. He felt a lump in his throat come up, and it took him a few moments to gather himself to continue. "Well, then. I will turn this over to Captain and Lt. Welch. Gentlemen," he said inclining his head towards them, and stepping back into line along with the rest of his men.

With that, Captain Welch stood before them hands on his hips. "Men, you're about to get dirty."

Chapter Sixteen

Clarissa looked up from the book she was reading aloud to see that the Duchess was sound asleep. She set the book down and tiptoed out of the bedchamber, shutting the door behind her. It was late afternoon, and she had stayed to read to Drusilla after their afternoon tea.

She hadn't seen David all day, and wondered how his meeting with the Welches had gone. As she descended the stairs, she thought she heard a commotion coming from outside. Rushing out towards the stables she saw all of the men of the estate, circled, and in the middle of it all were Lucas and Darius, seemingly beating upon each other. She was aghast as she saw Lucas heft his brother over his shoulder and heave him to the ground. Without thought she ran towards the circle of men.

"What is the meaning of this?" she demanded, pushing two footmen aside. She looked up to see David standing there, a look of bemusement on his face, which only angered her further. "Why aren't you stopping this?" she demanded of him.

"Miss Clarissa, it's not what you think." Darius interjected, struggling to his feet, brushing the dirt from his clothes. "We aren't fighting, we're training."

"Training? I just saw your brother grind you into the dirt. You could have been hurt!" she exclaimed. Darius looked affronted.

"He didn't grind me into the dirt. We were demonstrating a defensive combat maneuver. I knew what I was doing, and so did he," Darius defended.

"It's true. The Welches are training all of the men on the estate, to help with security." David assured her. "Now, this isn't a place for ladies, so perhaps you should go back to the house." He suggested. She crossed her arms and gave him a narrow eyed glare-a look he recalled from their childhood and he realized he had just made a tactical error.

"I will not go to the house! As you can see, by this plaster adorning my head, I am one of the people who needs to learn how to protect themselves, as well. If the Welch brothers are going to be kind enough to teach the men these things, then I want to learn, also." She insisted, giving him a look that dared him to stop her.

"Miss Clarissa, this isn't a place for a lady..." Darius objected, and she rounded on him. Darius had the foresight to take a step back. David knew he should object too, and insist that Clarissa remove herself, but realized that she did have a point. She had been the one who had ended up hurt when they were on the road; through no fault of her own She had the right to learn how to defend herself. He looked to Lucas.

"Lucas is leading this training. It is up to him, if you stay or go." David amended.

Lucas fixed him with a steely eyed glare, for putting him in the middle of Clarissa's ire. It was all David could do not to laugh. Finally, Lucas nodded and turned to Clarissa.

"I will teach you. Come here," he said, reluctantly. She walked to the center of the circle. Then Lucas motioned for David to come forward.

"As I was showing the men, when someone is coming at you, you can use their weight and momentum to your advantage." He did a slow motion demonstration, having Darius charge him. He ducked his shoulder under his brother, and turned as he grabbed his arm, flinging Darius to the ground, though much more gently this time. Clarissa nodded, absorbing what they were doing.

"Now, Your Grace, if you could come at Miss Clarissa." Lucas directed. David balked. He was worried he might hurt Clarissa and thought to deny his participation, but he saw the look on her face and realized she really did want to try, and he'd be damned if any of these other men would be partnered with her. He said a brief prayer that he didn't hurt her, or make a fool of himself, but did as instructed and charged at her. No one was more stunned than he was to find himself landing with an OOMPH hard on his back in the dirt. She had indeed flung him over her shoulder, and was now gleefully jumping up and down in joy and clapping her hands that she had accomplished the throw. He was too stunned to move. After a few moments, she stopped and looked down at him in concern.

"I didn't really hurt you, did I?" she asked, bending over him, and he could see the glee turning to worry. With as much dignity as possible, he hefted himself up off the ground and stood up, and realized a body slam to the ground was something he should put on his list of things to avoid in the future.

"I'm fine, fine," he insisted. He turned to the other men who all wore various expressions of amusement, although he gave them credit that none of them were laughing out loud. "See, gentlemen. If Miss Clarissa can do it, I have no doubt you can, too. Carry on," he said, then did his best not to hobble, as he walked towards a tack bench in the stable and sat down. Clarissa followed.

"Are you hurt? I am so sorry. I didn't really think I could do it. I'm quite surprised I did."

"I'm fine, I'm sure it amused Lucas and Darius to no end to see me flying through the air."

"I take it that your meeting today with them went well, as they are here."

"Very well, you were right; they are most capable men and know a great deal about protection and defense. They also have quite an operation going on their farm."

"They do. Darius has told me a bit about their plans. When they were in the service, they had a compatriot whose father owned a brewery and they spent some of their leave time there, and learned the process. I know Darius has read everything he can get his hands on about brewing and even has some ideas of improvements he can make on the machinery involved."

"You and Darius...you're friends, then?"

"Yes, I'd like to think so. When he left the service, he and Lucas were quite the pair. He couldn't walk at all, and Lucas could hardly see. I went to their place quite often to help them, brought them food and helped with chores that needed doing. They've returned the favor, several times over. When I have to go collect the rents, they've ridden with me, and I think that just having them back me up has kept all the tenants from giving excuses, or not paying."

"You've had to collect the rents? Why did I not know about this?" he asked.

"Your mother did it, up until last year, when

she became ill. You weren't here, and someone had to do it. I've enjoyed it. It has been good to get to know the tenants. You know, Lucas and Darius convinced a few of the farmers to change from wheat to hops, with the Duchess's blessing, of course. I sincerely hope this pays off for them. I have a feeling it will," she confided.

David sat in silence, thinking over her words. Once again, shame overwhelmed him. While he had been living the high-life in London, Clary had been here, basically fulfilling his duties and then some. He had avoided the estate for so many years, leaving his mother, and Clarissa to run it. Could he blame anyone for being skeptical of his skills, or leadership? He had known many men of the aristocracy who did nothing but go to balls and gamble, who had no care where their money was coming from, as long as it kept coming. He'd never really thought much about the tenants that resided on his land, or all that went into their day to day life. He'd never had to look any of them in the face, as he took from them, their hard earned money. He was ashamed to realize that today had been the first time he'd ever broken a sweat to help another person.

"The Welches are good men. Maybe...you should consider one of them." He suggested.

"Consider them for what?"

"Marriage."

"You seem quite anxious to marry me off, yet

again." She said drily.

"I'm not…I want you to be happy, that's all."

"I am. Well, except for people shooting me in the head. That was a bit disconcerting. And, the Duchess' illness, that is…difficult. You're home, and taking responsibility. That makes me happy. Especially when I have the chance to throw you about," she teased leaning against him, bumping his shoulder.

"I should be angry, as it was me who landed on their backside, but I am rather impressed. Proud, even. You did well, Clary," he told her and she smiled and he felt for the first time that the girl he had grown up with, the one who had been his best friend since birth was still there, and it gave him hope.

"I'm rather proud, too." She looked over to the assembled men who were now moving on to other hand to hand maneuvers. "Shall we join the throng again? Maybe I will get to do bodily harm to a Welch." She said cheekily.

"I can only hope," David laughed, and followed her back to the crowd.

Chapter Seventeen

They spent the remainder of the afternoon in training with the Welch brothers. David had learned boxing when he was in school, and often sparred with his friend, Kenton Fairchild, and a few others, so he had some experience. Still, he had to admit that the Welches were far superior in their knowledge of defense and fighting hand to hand.

The next day followed the same routine. He spent a few hours in the morning with his mother, going over the estate business. Then, with Robbie and Lawrence in tow, they proceeded to the Welch's farm to help them with their tasks. This day they worked on the framework of the building for their brewing room. David looked over their plans and made a few suggestions that the Welch's agreed would be better.

They worked into the afternoon, and then proceeded back to Hollister House to continue the men's training. As expected Clarissa joined them without hesitation. David knew better than to object.

This time they went over how to use a knife in combat. He was a bit disturbed that the only person who picked up throwing a knife effectively on the first try, was Clarissa, although he could hardly be surprised. Their whole lives, she had always picked up things rather quickly, and had a natural athletic ability. He might be stronger than her, but he had no doubt that in a footrace, she could still outrun him or shoot a gun or an arrow or throw a knife more accurately. Still, she never lorded it over him, and he had given her plenty of opportunities over the years as they were growing up.

Everyone was taking turns at the makeshift knife target which had been drawn on the side of the stable.

As Clarissa had gone first, she had stepped to the side, and Darius Welch wandered over and they spoke in low tones. David watched them out of the corner of his eye, saw how Darius bent close to hear what Clarissa had to say, saw how she smiled up at him and he smiled back. He had liked Darius on first meeting, but in that moment he wanted nothing more than to punch him in the face.

David's turn to throw at the target came up again and he picked up the knife and imagined Darius as the dead center of the target and heaved it forward. He nailed the center of the bullseye. Clarissa cheered and applauded and he felt himself blush at her enthusiasm, but also felt buoyed by the small achievement. He stepped aside as the next man took his turn and Clarissa came up to him.

"You have quite the knack with a knife," Clarissa said.

"So do you. As I recall you hit the bullseye on your first throw." He commented. She shrugged, as if it were nothing.

"Things like that, I am good at. Not the important things."

"What do you mean?"

"Women are supposed to sew, and paint and play the pianoforte, sing. I could never master any of it, and could not even summon the desire to. I remember after you left for Eton, it seemed my mother and your mother was determined to make a lady of me. None of their lessons quite took. I always felt like I was a disappointment to both of them," she confided. He could only look at her in shock.

"You can't think that. I highly doubt either of them was disappointed," he assured.

"You know, your mother actually offered to sponsor me for a season. She was going to declare that I was her niece, and give me the opportunity to make a match." Clarissa told him. He was surprised by the information. To think he could have seen her at balls and events, like any of the other debutantes of the ton. He could just imagine if they had met under such circumstances. He would have delighted in courting her.

"Why didn't you do it?"

"I've never had much desire for those things, balls and dances and house parties. It always seemed like such frippery. It's a life that would have made me miserable. I like it here, the quiet of the garden and the woods. I like knowing every single person I see by name, when I go into the village. I don't know how you do it."

"It's part of having the title. I have been to any number of balls in the last few years; one is very much like another. I usually do a few turns around the dance floor with the hosts' wife or daughter then spends the rest of the evening playing cards."

"You do not go seeking the ladies?" she asked. He looked at her.

"I usually spend such events doing my level best to avoid them, and their mothers. You have no idea what it is like to hear yourself announced 'Duke of Hollister' and suddenly see a swarm of muslin and satin coming at you. There are some events I've barely escaped intact," he declared, shuddering. Clarissa laughed and he basked in the sound.

"You are quite brave to put yourself in such dangerous circumstances."

"You have no idea," he agreed.

Lucas Welch pulled the knife from the target one last time, and addressed all of the men present, including Clarissa. He went over a schedule for guarding the perimeter, explaining he and Darius would also take turns guarding the property at night. He paired the rest of them up to guard during the day. He warned them to be especially leery of strangers, or anyone asking questions about Hollister House or the Duke, and to report such immediately.

David took over at this point, advising they would meet the same time tomorrow, finally adjourning the group.

David approached the Welches and asked if they would like to stay for supper. They both looked down at their sweaty, dusty attire and declined. David assured them they would be welcome and would have time to make themselves presentable if they wished to. Reluctantly they accepted. He turned to Clarissa, "You'll dine with us, of course."

"I'm not sure it's appropriate…"

"Nonsense. It's my table and I can decide who dines at it. You are dining with us," he insisted. She rolled her eyes at his audacity and he had to grin. He had her.

"I would be delighted. I shall likewise, go and make myself presentable." She told them, bowing her head towards the Welches. "Gentlemen," she said, making her leave.

All three men stood and watched her flounce her way into the house. David did not feel he imagined the extra sway to her hips as she seemed to know all the men had their eyes on her. He just had to wonder which one she had a wish to attract.

The Welches, likewise, made their leave and David let Franklin know that there would be four for dinner that night in two hours' time. He also asked a bath be drawn for him. He bathed and readied for the evening, putting on fresh clothes and even bothering to put on a cravat and a dinner jacket. He realized he was actually looking forward to the coming evening. The Welches were not titled gentlemen, to be sure, but he liked and respected them, even Darius, despite the fact that he had an eye for Clarissa. He wanted to thank them for their assistance and also hear more about the brewery venture they were planning. He had a few ideas of how it could be promoted about the ton. He knew that the upper echelons of society, especially the moneyed of the set, always had a desire for the latest and greatest thing. He would just need to convince them that the Welches beer was the thing. He could get Fairchild in on it, too. Kenton always fancied himself the bellwether of their set, and seemed to do quite well with his own business endeavors. David had no doubt he could help the Welch's launch their beer to the upper Ten Thousand in London with little effort. With that thought in mind, he made his way to the salon, just as the Welches arrived.

Both men had freshened up and wore clean clothes, and freshly polished boots and worn, but presentable jackets. Both had their overly long hair combed back and in a que, and were clean shaven. Quite the feat compared to how they had looked earlier. He was just offering them drinks when Clarissa showed up in the doorway. Darius noticed her first, his eyes widening dramatically and his mouth gaping open, followed by Lucas who raised not one, but both of his eyebrows in surprise. David hesitated, his back was to the door, but when he turned he could see what both men were gawking at. Clarissa had dressed for dinner in a dress of the palest blue satin, with delicate lace edging the bodice and cap sleeves. It was cut low, and her bosom looked quite delectable on display. She wore her normally straight hair half up and half down, with a crown of curls atop her head and spirals of curls down her back and over her shoulder, as if perfectly framing her assets. Her tiny waist was cinched in and she wore delicate white lace gloves that went to her elbow, leaving a delectable bit of arm bare. Her lips were tinted like cherries, and her eyes stood out in her face with a bit of kohl applied to her lashes. He had always thought Clarissa was pretty, but he had no idea that she could be so breathtakingly beautiful. He didn't realize he was gawking until he saw a look of self-consciousness cross her face and she took a hesitant step back. That brought him out of the beauty induced stupor and he stepped forward.

"Miss Clarissa, you are looking lovely," he assured her. She smiled hesitantly, a becoming blush coming to her cheeks and looked beyond him to Darius and Lucas and smiled at the other two men.

"You look very handsome tonight. I don't have the opportunity to dress up very often but I felt the company deserved my best efforts," she said, inclining her head to all of them. Darius stepped forward and brought her gloved hand to his lips and kissed her knuckles.

"The Duke is indeed correct, you are looking most lovely and your efforts are most appreciated." He said, lingering over her hand. Lucas, not to be outdone by his brother also bowed to her and kissed her knuckles.

"You do look lovely tonight, Miss Clarissa," he said solemnly then ruined it with a wink of his good eye. She laughed, as she was supposed to, and at once felt relaxed. David poured a glass for each of them and no sooner had they finished their drinks when Franklin announced dinner. David extended his arm to Clarissa to escort her to the dining room. At first she looked at his arm, as if unsure what to do, then with a bit of hesitation, took it and let him lead her into the dining room.

It wasn't the first time she had dined with either David, or the Welch brothers. When she was a child, their mothers often dined with them and it was very much like a family, she and Annabelle and David and the Duchess. She knew in most households of the realm, children did not dine with their elders, and certainly servants did not dine with their masters but it seemed that the lines had always been a bit blurred at Hollister House. David had been raised to be a Duke, but could just as easily dine and converse with the common man.

Clarissa wasn't sure what she was expecting of the evening. When David had asked her to dine with him and the Welch's, she wondered if there was some ulterior motive behind it. But, it had been some time since she had dined in the company of men and decided to put her best foot forward. She borrowed the hot crimping iron that she had often used on the Duchess, and pulled a dress out of the back of her closet. Drusilla had ordered it for her twenty first birthday. She had worn it on that event, hoping against hope that David would come home for their shared birthday celebration, but he had not. She and the

Duchess had dined alone and Clarissa tried to tell herself that she was not hurt by his disregard. Tonight she had seen the appreciation in his eyes and was glad that she had gone to the trouble to look nice for the gentlemen present.

Wine was poured and the first course came out. She saw the Welches look hesitantly at the array of dishes and silverware at the table. She made a point of being obvious when she took the fork from the far outside of the cutlery displayed so they would know which one to use. David, of course, was oblivious to their discomfort. Knowing which fork to use and proper etiquette in all matters was second nature to him. She wondered if she had been raised as the proper daughter of the Duke if she would be likewise just as oblivious. She hoped not. She recalled their lessons in deportment as children. She had taken easily to it, where David had struggled along. She knew that the reason he had stuck with it at all was because she did. She also knew that the Duchess had drummed it into him that he was the Duke of Hollister and had an image to uphold. She had tried to instill him with pride of that position, but instead it only built up a bitter resentment. He now seemed resigned to his position, she so hoped he would find contentment as the Duke.

They spent the meal talking over the plans for security, as well as the future plans for the Welches operation. The brothers were hardworking, ambition, and intelligent.

Clarissa was quite familiar with Darius, he was a voracious reader and years earlier the Duchess had told him he could borrow any book from the estates library. He took her at her word, and had plowed through the contents of most of the shelves. The Duchess had even ordered some books for him on the craft of brewing and had been dismayed when they arrived in Prussian. Darius simply borrowed a book of definitions and taught himself the language. She made a remark about that during dinner and was surprised to see Darius blush

"He has not told you his secret?" Lucas asked.

"Secret?"

"I...remember things. Books I've read maps, drawings, numbers, it came in quite handy in the service, and I could memorize battle plans and then deliver them without worry of them being discovered. I carried the information in my head."

"That's quite remarkable," David commented.

"So you really were able to learn Prussian from reading a book?" Clarissa asked in amazement.

"Two books actually, the first was little more than a children's primer."

"I have read everything there is to know about the growing and brewing process. The equipment we have ordered should be arriving anytime but I have ideas about how to improve it.

One of the downfalls of the brewing process is the lack of cooling. I have thought of a way to rapidly cool the brew which in turn would preserve the flavor to a greater extent. I am anxious to experiment with that."

"I wish you the best of luck with that. My mother has great faith in your endeavor and I think I am following her lead. I would be happy to be of any assistance I can," David offered. Clarissa sent him a beaming smile and he had to stop himself from giving an equally smitten grin in return.

"We appreciate that, Your Grace," Lucas acknowledged.

Surprisingly the conversation around the table was quite lively. The Welches each complimented her on her throwing skills, with knives as well as with men. David gallantly offered to step aside as her practice partner so the Welches could evaluate her skills properly, from the ground. With grins, the gentlemen politely declined, claiming he was obviously the better partner in this case. They discussed the future plans for the brewery and spoke about harvest schedules and the various things that needed to be accomplished. David seemed quite enthused with the endeavor and it appeared that he fully intended to be invested in the project. He shared his own ideas with marketing the beer, which were well received.

After dinner they all adjourned to the library, and chatted well into the evening. Clarissa wasn't sure what she had expected but she was quite delighted to find that a genuine respect and friendship seemed to be growing between the Welch brothers and David. That night Darius left for home and Lucas stayed, as promised and guarded the house. She said her good-nights and went to bed.

The evening was rather warm, and she opened her window a few inches and could hear the Lucas and David outside, talking, sometimes laughing softly as if jesting with each other. She drifted off to sleep, with the sound of a happy David in her ears.

Chapter Eighteen

The next day, David spent his morning with the Duchess. She spent a few hours carefully going over the various investments with him. He had to admit that she was a shrewd business woman and had done a remarkable job growing the family fortune. She had much advice over matters she felt he should invest in, in the future. She was quite interested in the idea of train travel and was insistent that at the first opportunity, that David had to invest in a rail line to the area from London, he should leap at the opportunity. She foresaw a future where people could travel from London or other parts of the country in just a few hours instead of days, and that people might someday like to holiday in the area, taking in the bucolic hills and scenery. He promised he would look into it as soon as he was able. As it were, he could only dream of traveling to and from London in a matter of hours, instead of the normal two-day jaunt.

The night before Lucas had told him that he

was going to the next county to pick up more building supplies, and Darius had offered to help Robbie and MacPherson fix the broken gate to the enclosure around the stable. This left him with a free afternoon, once he and the Duchess concluded their morning talk.

Halfway through the session with his mother, Clarissa joined them. She sat quietly, saying very little. Still he was aware of her presence, like a divining rod his body seemed to seek hers out and want to edge closer, and closer to hers. After a while it was evident that the Duchess' energy was flagging. Clarissa took charge and insisted she rest. Together they helped her up to her room. David assured his mother they could pick up where they left off when he came back for tea, and for once, his mother did not argue. She was drifting off to sleep before he and Clarissa even left the room.

Clarissa closed his mother's bedroom door behind her, and they stood looking at each other in the hallway. The air between them suddenly felt heavy. His fingers itched to cover the distance between them and touch her skin, her face, and her lips. To take her in his arms, knowing that Clarissa's room was just twenty feet away, and his own, in the next wing over, he wisely stepped back, and clasped his hands behind his back, searching his mind for a topic that was not too intimate.

"Is our tree-house still standing?" He asked. Her eyebrows shot up in surprise, and then a smile curled her lips.

"Last I saw it, it was, although I have to admit that was months ago. It has to have been three summers since I've had use of it," she admitted.

"Let's go have a look then," he challenged. They made their way down the stairs and went outside, cutting through the garden to where it edged the woods. The path that they had taken on a near daily basis as children was now quite grown over, and every once in a while they needed to step and brush aside a branch or debris to continue on.

The tree came into sight, a sturdy oak that had probably been there for hundreds of years. The tree-house was neatly hidden within its canopy of leaves. One might not even know it was there except for the rope ladder hanging down, and if you looked straight up, when standing at the base of the trunk, the platform could be discerned.

David placed his foot on the bottom rung of the rope ladder and bounced a few times to test its sturdiness. It held up nicely, and he smiled, stepping down. He gave a royal bow to Clarissa, and she smiled.

"Ladies first," he said. She gave him an answering grin and quickly, hitched her skirt over one arm and scrambled up the ladder. He did his best not to ogle her bared ankles and calves, as he waited his turn to ascend the rope ladder as well. For a moment he questioned the wisdom of doing this, being alone this way. They were no longer children after all. Still, Clarissa had not hesitated to join him on this adventure and he did not have the heart to call her back down. He waited until she reached the top before making his own way up. The platform had a railing on all sides, and the leaves of the tree were almost like walls. Above it was a generous opening to the sky.

He recalled one summer night, shortly before he left for Eton, when he and Clarissa had come out here, laid a blanket down and simply gazed up at the stars. Spending hours talking, he remembered how she had tentatively reached out and taken his hand in hers and then laid her head on his shoulder. It had been the first time in his young life that he had felt the awareness of her, an awakening of feelings that were more than brotherly, or friendly.

He'd been so happy that night, blissfully happy with her small hand in his and her head lying trustingly against his shoulder. In his early days at Eton, on nights when he was especially homesick, he'd thought about that night, when everything was perfect, and they were the only two people in the world.

She walked carefully about the platform, testing its durability. "A bit creaky, here or there but it seems to be in decent shape. There's a board or two that might need replacing and maybe we should reinforce the railing with a few nails," she suggested. She crouched down and brushed a layer of dead leaves and acorns off a section of the platform. The debris rained down to the ground landing with a soft whooshing sound against the forest floor. She sat down on the cleared space. He likewise did the same, and sat down, leaning against one side of the tree trunk.

"It's much smaller than I remember," he commented.

"I don't think it's much smaller, I think that we are much bigger. We were all of ten years old when we built this."

"With MacPherson's help, we'd have never gotten the platform into the tree without his assistance." he said, remembering the day they had enlisted his aid to pull the platform up on a pulley, and place it just so that it rested flat against two of the tree boughs. He'd also secured a few braces hammered into the tree underneath to ensure that the platform could not shift or move.

"I still wish we had built a second one in that tree over there and built that rope bridge across." He said pointing to the twin oak, not fifteen feet away. They had ambitiously talked about it, but then he had left for Eton, and when he came back the following summer, she seemed to have lost interest in the idea and so he never brought it up again.

"Maybe you can do that for your own children, someday," she said. She was looking out towards the other tree, as if imagining the opposite platform and the rope bridge that could exist between them.

David tried to picture his own children; he could envision a boy with his own curly dark hair and Clarissa's blue eyes and bright smile, or maybe a blond haired girl with a dimple like his in her cheek. He was lost in thought when he realized that Clarissa was sniffling. He looked at her, surprised to see tears in her eyes. He scooted closer to her, and put his arm around her. He thought for a second she would pull away, but she didn't. With a resigned sigh she dropped her head against his shoulder.

"What's wrong?" he asked.

"You're going to have children someday," she whispered, brokenly.

"Will I?"

"You will...but I won't."

"Why don't you think you'll have children?" he asked, it seemed that the air around them had suddenly gone still, and he felt in that moment all the walls between them had come down. He waited for her to answer. She wiped her face with the back of her sleeve and took a deep breath, then looked him in the eye.

"I will never have children, because the only person I'd want them with, is you. It can never happen," she told him. He gasped at her declaration, feeling an overwhelming joy. She still wanted him, as he wanted her.

"Clary. . .I can't imagine having a child with any other woman, then you," he admitted. "I have tried, for nearly a decade to suppress any feelings I have for you, but God...there is only you, for me."

"A Duke cannot marry a maid, it isn't done," she protested, although the protest sounded weak to both of their ears.

"A Duke can marry whom he pleases, and the rest of the world be damned," he declared. He remembered his mother's arguments against this, but he no longer gave them any credence. Clarissa was a strong, intelligent woman; she would not be cowed by the insipid ladies of the ton. Anyone who would not accept her as his wife would find themselves excluded from his considerable circle.

If there was one thing he'd learned in the last few years, it was that everyone wanted his approval, whether they were deserving of it, or not. He was not at the mercy of the ton, as much as they were at the mercy of him. There was a certain power in that, and he intended to use it.

"You can't mean that. You have to think of your legacy. You must find a lady of good breeding, from the right circles. I am your mother's ladies' maid and companion, I do not qualify," she insisted.

"Clary, what of what I want, what I feel? Does that matter to no one? Does that not matter to you?"

"It can't. It doesn't matter what I feel either. It just isn't done. It cannot be," she insisted tearfully. She seemed adamant to resist the idea of marriage to him, so he used the only other way to persuade her that he could think of. He leaned down and tilted her chin up to with a finger and kissed her.

The kiss seemed to stun her, for a moment she did not respond, then it was as if the floodgates released and she turned into his embrace and wrapped her arms around his neck, and opened her sweet mouth to his, responding fully. Without releasing her mouth, he pulled her closer until she was straddling his lap. For several minutes they were lost in each other, one kiss lead to another, and another.

A smooth adjustment of her dress and he could feel her pressed against him, he cursed the barrier of clothes between them, and she seemed to writhe in frustration, needing something more, grinding against him, trying to get closer, trying to find release. He slipped a hand between them, between her legs and found that spot. She broke the kiss, and seemed to lean back, but that only pressed her more firmly against his fingers, her breath heaving. He could see the war on her face between intense desire and protest. He'd be damned if he'd let her run away. He held her firmly in place with his left hand and redoubled his efforts with his right. The sound of her gasps and moans were almost enough to set him off her eyes drifted shut, he could feel her thighs quaking, could feel the core of her go tight.

"Look at me!" he demanded "I want to see the fire in your eyes."

Her eyes flew open and locked onto his, and she cried out, nearly screaming and he felt her quim spasm, against his hand, and her whole body quake against his. He watched it all on her face from agonizing pleasure to finally, contented calm bliss. She slumped forward; her body seemed to melt against his. She had found her release, but he was still in a state of crazed arousal.

He desperately wanted to lay her down and feel her thighs wrapped around him and slide into the hot core of her and find his release. He was literally throbbing from want of her, only her. When he felt her hand at the buttons of his falls, he knew he should stop her. Once released, he wasn't sure he would have the power not to take her. She slid off his lap and pushed him onto his back. Leaves and twigs poked into him, but he did not care. She finished unbuttoning his breeches and reached inside with shaking hands, pulling his cock free. She sat back on her heels and looked at it in amazement. Then she met his eyes and grinned, a blush coming to her cheeks.

"It was so dark that night; I never really got a good look at it. I didn't realize...it's a bit bigger than I remember." She said her fingers explored him, relearning the texture of warm satin covered steel. She caressed him and he closed his eyes in exquisite agony, gritting his teeth, and willing himself not to explode at her tender touch.

When she grew bold and grasped him firmly in her fist he wanted to shout in exultation. She smoothed her thumb over the weeping slit at the top and spread the moisture down. Realizing she needed more lubricant than that, she spit in her hand and returned to her task. He groaned as she sped up the pace of her strokes and his balls seized, ready to let loose.

"Look at me," she demanded. "I want to see the fire in your eyes." He hadn't even realized his eyes were still closed but he did as she bid and opened them, looking straight into hers as his cock found release within her grasp. Her own eyes showed her shock and amazement as he cried out and spurt after spurt erupted, covering her hand and landing in the leaves around them.

He slumped back, his chest heaving. He was vaguely aware of her pulling a handkerchief from the pocket of her dress and wiping her hand, then him clean. He reached for her, not even bothering to set himself right and button up. Without a word she nestled against his chest, within the circle of his arms and for several minutes they lay in contented silence. Suddenly He felt something light hit his arm, a few seconds later; Clarissa jerked she felt a similar projectile against her shoulder. They both looked up just as a squirrel in a nearby branch launched another acorn in their direction which bounced off Clarissa's head and caught David squarely on the chin.

"We're under attack!" Clarissa laughed shielding her head. David cursed the squirrel but even he could see the humor in the situation.

"Apparently our amorous activities have offended the Lord Squirrel." He surmised. They both sat up and he struggled back into his breeches, buttoning up as two more acorn missiles came his way, one nicking him in the ear. "Best we vacate before he calls in reinforcements." Hastily they made their way down the rope ladder. Once reaching the ground he took her hand in his, and instead of taking the path back towards Hollister House, he went the opposite direction, towards the lake.

Chapter Nineteen

Clarissa forgot what a wonder it was to walk hand in hand with David. It was something they had done as children. In the afternoons, when their lessons were done and their governess was napping and their mothers occupied in their parlor, David would give her a look and crook his chin towards the door, then grabbed her by the hand and they would take off towards the woods beyond the garden.

Her favorite destination was the lake, which in all actuality was more of a pond. If the weather was warm they would strip down to their underclothes and swim. If it was cool they would simply sit side by side on the big flat boulder that rested on the eastern edge of the lake and try to best each other at skipping stones across its surface.

They reached the lake and made their way to the boulder. The boulder was about four feet off the ground, and just as they had done as they were children, David climbed up first, then bent and reached a hand to help Clarissa up onto it. This time when he pulled her up, he continued until she was in his arms. She knew she should protest, step away, but there was no point in denying that the only place she ever wanted to be was David's embrace.

She leaned her head against his chest, secretly thrilled at how she fit just under his chin. How his body seemed made to cradle hers against it. With a sigh, she stepped away and sat down on the edge of the stone platform, facing the lake. He sat down beside her.

He picked up a flat stone and cast it out. It skipped across the surface twice before sinking. He picked up another stone, handing it to Clarissa. She threw it, and it skipped four times. David rolled his eyes and gave her a quirking respectful smile at her superior cast.

"I see you've been practicing."

"Not in a while. I use to bring Robbie out here when he was younger, and taught him how to skip stones. He's actually quite good. I saw him make seven skips once. It's been ages though, at least a few years."

"What made you stop coming?"

"Well...I think at some point I felt young Robbie had begun to develop...a romantic feeling towards me and it was best to discourage that."

"I'm not surprised. I don't think there is a man on earth who could resist the thought of you. Although it's funny that you would bring Robbie here, at all, he was most likely conceived on this spot." David laughed.

Clarissa shot him a startled glance, then joined in his laughter, remembering the day they had come across a teenage MacPherson and Betty on this very boulder, in the midst of a passionate interlude.

"I've endeavored to forget about that. How old were we? Seven or so? I don't know who was more shocked, them or us."

"I can still picture Mac, struggling to pull up his breeches, and Betty screeching at us to turn away. And you were all questions, "Mac, why were you lying on top of Betty? And why is your face so red?" he recalled in a mocking falsetto.

"Well, I didn't know! I hadn't a clue what they were doing, although I have a much better idea now."

"As a recall they married a month later in May, and Robbie was born in January."

"It is rude to count months. It's best to assume he was born early."

"I shall not comment on that. I do remember feeling quite put out that they sullied my favorite spot, with their amorous activities. Of course, at seven the idea of kissing girls was the most repugnant thing I could imagine. I thought it better to kiss a frog than a female."

"It's apparent you've changed your mind on

that score." She commented.

"Have I? Maybe I need a bit more convincing." He enticed.

"I thought I did a fine job convincing you earlier." She said drily.

"Maybe it is I who ought to be convincing you, then." He said capturing her lips against his. At the first touch of his mouth she felt a sizzle of heat and her breath escaped her. He cupped her face in his hands and continued kissing her, first her mouth, then skimmed her jaw and found a spot on the side of her neck that simply had her catching her breath. He nipped at that spot with his teeth and she gasped, clutching his shoulders. She wanted him, not just his hands on her, and hers on him. She wanted to take him inside herself and know what it was truly like to be one, with David. Something she couldn't even fathom wanting with any other man. With a tremendous effort she pulled away from him, and took a moment to catch her breath.

"We dare not take this any further. We don't want to be scandalizing the next generation of children that might come upon us," he quipped.

"I wouldn't call it scandalizing so much as educating. A good education is to be prized. Isn't that what the Duchess always said?"

"Well then I suggest you ask the Duchess what she thinks of you educating me in this way, and see if she agrees." She said primly. He gave a telling harumph.

"You certainly know the way to put a damper on my desire. Thoughts of my mother are the last thing I want to be thinking about when I am with you."

"Maybe I should carry your mother's portrait about to keep you at bay," she teased.

"No need of that. I can be a gentleman," he assured. She raised a smirking eyebrow, and he laughed. "Well, I can try! It isn't my fault you are so beautiful and tempting."

"You are a man full of delusions. I am passably pretty at best." She denied his compliment with a shake of her head.

"Now it is you who are delusional. Or have you not passed a looking glass in years? My dear, you are beautiful, and I am not just saying that. You would be the envy of every woman of the ton."

"My hair is straight as a stick and the color of straw, and I have freckles about my nose. And one front tooth is a bit crooked," she protested.

"Your hair is a waterfall of gold, and your freckles are delectable, the front tooth isn't noticeable at all, because when you smile all one sees is the way it lights up your face, and everything else in the world falls away," he declared. She tried to discern if he was mocking her, but his words were said with all sincerity. "The most beautiful thing about you," he continued, "is that you have no idea how truly lovely you are."

"Oh," she breathed.

"You think I'm just having you on?"

"No...no. I believe that you believe what you are saying," she assured him.

"You just do not believe that it is true. Someday, I will convince you."

"Maybe, you will." She thought about his words. She felt humbled and oddly exhilarated. David thought she was beautiful, or as he said, truly lovely.

For years while she had been here at Hollister, she had thought about him being away, first at Eton, then Cambridge, and then London. She had wondered at all the girls and women he was meeting, and had been so jealous and envious of these ladies who vied for his attention. She was certain they were all more attractive, more worldly than she was.

She had spent a lifetime watching him leave, time and time again. She had tried to protect herself, by treating him with deference, pretending to be indifferent to him. He declared that he was home to stay. But could she believe that? As soon as the Duchess passed, there would be nothing really keeping him here. Would he return again to London, and leave her behind, yet again? She wanted to believe that he was sincere, that he wanted her, wanted to build a life with her.

These last few days, things had changed so much between them. They had found a way back to their old camaraderie. But there was something more, something different.

"I can see the wheels turning in your head over there." He said. "Tell me what you're thinking."

"I'm wondering when you will leave again," she answered honestly.

"I told you, I'm not leaving. I'm here to stay."

"Until you're bored, then you will go, like you always do," she said sadly. She skipped another stone towards the lake, but it didn't skip at all, just sunk.

"Is that what you think, every time I've left, that it was because I was bored?"

"I don't know. You'd come back, and each time I would think maybe this time you would stay, and every time, within a few days you'd be gone. Every time it would be like when...Never mind. This is a silly conversation," she said. She got up, and leapt off the rock, to the ground, striding quickly towards the path to the house. She heard him scramble to follow her. He grabbed her by the shoulder, stopping her, and turned her to face him.

"Wait," he said, "every time it would be like what? What are you talking about?"

She kept her eyes firmly on the ground. God, she never wanted to talk about that. She felt her cheeks burn with the humiliation of that moment in her life, when she had been such a fool.

"It isn't important," she insisted. "We should

be getting back."

"I beg to differ. It appears to be very important. Please tell me. Clary, you can tell me anything." He swore, he hooked a finger under her chin and tilted her face so that her eyes met his. She saw only confusion, and worry there, and a yearning to understand. She felt tears prick her eyes, and felt something inside her crack.

"You...you left me," she whispered, brokenly. "That...that night we spent together, when we were sixteen, I thought it was just the beginning, you see. I was so sure; I wanted to believe you so badly. I heard you tell your mother you wanted to marry me. She told me...she told me you couldn't have meant it, that you were caught up in the moment and would come to regret what happened, and I didn't believe her. I was so certain, you'd stay, or if you left you'd insist I come with you. But you didn't...you left me," she accused with anguished cry. She swiped a hand across her eyes, to obliterate the tears that were starting to fall, she took a breath, and he waited, in silence, sensing there was much more she needed to say. "David, my mother was dead, I had no one. No one, except you, and you left. I had told you I loved you, but it didn't stop you. You still left me behind." She was sobbing by the time the last word left her lips.

In horror she covered her mouth with her fingers, wishing she could recall those words. She had never wanted him to know how devastated she had been at his abandonment. How even now, eight years later, she still feared he would desert her, yet again, and she feared when he did, she would never recover.

"Is that what you think, that I left you, without a thought? If I did not leave, the Duchess threatened to send you away, and I had no doubt that she would. I had to go. Besides, I was still in school; I still had a year left at Eton, then. I knew if I ever wanted a future with you, I needed my education. I wrote to you, to explain, to ask you to wait, but you refused to respond to any of my letters."

"You wrote me?"

"Yes, practically every day after I left, but you never responded. Then when I came back at the break, you were so distant. You looked right through me, wouldn't even be alone with me so I could talk to you. God Clary, it broke my heart."

"I never received any letters. I know your mother received letters from you, but you never wrote to me. I was so hurt, we'd always been such friends and then that night, I felt like I'd lost your friendship too. I thought you regretted our being together."

"Regretted it? My God Clary, that night was everything to me. The aftermath was what devastated me. I thought you regretted it, and that you hated me for it."

"I could never hate you," she whispered. "You really wrote to me?"

"I did, I promise. My mother must have kept the letters from you," he guessed.

"I suspect you could be right about that."

"Each time I came back; you were so...cold. So indifferent, it hurt so much that I couldn't bear it. It was easier to be gone than to be near you, knowing you no longer wanted me."

"And each time you would leave it was like proof that you had no care for me..."

"We were both so wrong. I feel a fool for not confronting you years ago about this, or confronting my mother. I am so angry with her for keeping us apart all this time."

"I'm sure she did it thinking she was doing the right thing. We were very young, too young to think about marriage, and she is still right, you are a Duke, and I am still someone in service. We are not meant to be."

"You can't still believe that! We can start over, be together. You want to be with me, I know you do."

"That still doesn't make it right. We are from different worlds," she reasoned.

"Different worlds? We were raised in the same house, not a hundred feet apart, ate at the same table, born on the same day, for God's sake! How can you even think that we do not belong together? I refuse, refuse to believe that! I am not walking away from you a second time!" he insisted, taking her by the shoulders.

"Well then, maybe it is I who will do the walking away this time," she said. She turned out of his grasp, and started down the path. It was several seconds before a stunned David was at her side.

"You do not mean that. I know you don't," he declared. She cast him a look over her shoulder. She wasn't sure what she meant but she knew that she was not going to get caught up in passion, only to be crushed again as he rode away.

"Clarissa, where are you going?"

"Back to the house."

"Don't be this way. Let's talk and sort this out," he insisted.

She kept on walking, ignoring him as best as she could, although he kept an even stride beside her, only dropping back when the narrow path through the woods demanded it. As soon as they cleared the woods, she picked up her skirts and took off running. She felt David on her heels but didn't dare look back. She just knew she had to get away, get to her room and shut and locked the door before she gave in to all the emotions that seemed to be crushing in on her from all sides. Her foot caught on something and she pitched forward, her hands extended to save herself from the fall. Before she could hit the ground, she felt David's arms come around her, and he stumbled to the ground, but turned her so he took the brunt of the fall and she landed atop him, unhurt.

"Damn it, woman! Stop running away from me," he demanded, wrapping his arms about her like steel bands. She fought to get away from him and he rolled her over so that she was lying in the grass, and he braced her hands over her head and used his lower body to anchor her in place. She struggled against him, but he calmly waited her out, finally. She stopped and he relaxed his grip on her.

"I don't like being manhandled," she said petulantly.

"Well then stop fighting and trying to run away. Talk to me, Clary."

"I'm just...angry. Upset. The Duchess, she...let me live a lie for years. Years! And to what end? To keep me like a dog at her side? I don't even know. I want so badly to have it out with her, but she is dying. And what kind of person would I be to go ranting at a dying woman?" Her voice vibrated with frustration.

"I know. All we can do is go forward. We know the truth now. We can start over, be together." He reasoned.

"No...this doesn't change anything."

"Clary, do you think I could give you up now? After feeling your kisses? After knowing what it is like to feel you come undone in my arms? The feel of your mouth on me...you would give me a taste of paradise and cruelly it takes away, to what end?" he pleaded.

"I should never have let you kiss me again."

"It was inevitable. I could not stay away from you anymore than I could stop breathing. You're in my blood." He said dipping his head he kissed her gently. Her eyelids fluttered closed and he kissed each one, tasting the tears that still fell.

"I want to believe in you." She said honestly. "I need time."

"I can give you that. I'll give you anything you want, Clary." He released her wrists, and brought each one up to his mouth to kiss it. With a sigh, he pushed himself up then extended a hand to her, to help her up. He did not release her hand, however, once she was on her feet. He linked his fingers with hers and together they walked back to the house.

As they neared the house, she saw Darius, on horseback, talking to Robbie at the stable. Both seemed to go still as a statue, at seeing her and David walking hand in hand. She tried to pull her hand away from David's but he held it fast. She glanced up to see a look of sad resignation on Darius's face and wide eyed shock on Robbie's. "Gentlemen," she said dipping her head. Darius gave them a nod, and turned away from her and addressed David.

"Your Grace, might I have a word with you? Regarding the security training."

"Of course," David reluctantly let go of Clarissa's hand. "I'll see you at tea with Mother." He said to her. She left them to go back into the house, alone, and tried to ignore the feeling of three pairs of eyes, on her back.

Chapter Twenty

Clarissa had been staring at the chessboard for some time without really seeing it. David was with Lucas and Darius, leaving her alone with the duchess in her bedchamber parlor. Her mind kept circling back to the talk she and David had, coming back from the lake.

"I can see your mind is not on the game, Clarissa. May I ask what is troubling you so?" the Duchess finally asked. Clarissa thought first to say nothing, what good could come of bringing up such sordid things now? But her curiosity won out.

"David asked me today, why I never responded to any of the letters he wrote to me, when he went back to school, after we were together." She said finally. "I told him the truth. That I had never received any letters."

"I see," The Duchess finally said.

"Your Grace...why?" She struggled for words, finally giving up and letting the question hang in the air. The Duchess looked away and fumbled with the hem of the blanket that covered her lap. Clarissa waited her out.

"I thought, at the time, it was the right thing to do."

"You thought I was not good enough for him?" Clarissa guessed.

The Duchess's eyes widened in shock and she shook her head, "No Clarissa, you know that isn't true." After several moments, the duchess seemed to come to some decision. "First, I want you to know that I thought I was protecting you. You were both so young. I was worried that it was a childish infatuation for both of you, and that you'd both regret it, if it continued. That is why I interfered. In hindsight, I should have realized it was more serious."

"You say you were protecting me, but I think you were also protecting yourself," Clarissa declared. She waited for the Duchess to deny it, but she didn't."

"Perhaps, I was. We had just lost Annabelle, and David was already out in the world. I feared you would leave me, too. So selfishly, I kept his letters from you. I thought...I thought in time you would get over it. That he would get over it. I have regretted it. I feel that David has always blamed me for your estrangement, and never forgiven me for it. And you...whenever he would visit, and then leave you would sulk for days. Had I any idea, I would have handled things differently."

"If...if we wanted to be together now, would you approve?" Clarissa had to ask.

"I wouldn't stand in your way. Not now. What would be the point? I'll be gone soon enough and you will both be making your own decisions."

"I don't know that this makes everything right. What you said back then was true. To the world he is a Duke, and I am merely a ladies' maid and companion. What business do we have being together? Who would respect such a union?"

The Duchess reached across and clasped her hand. "The people who mattered, would. Besides, we both know you aren't just a ladies' maid, and never were. Some things are more important than rank and titles and wealth. It has taken me a lifetime to realize that. Love, my darling girl, love is more important than any of it. If there is one lesson that I've learned, in dying, it is that. The rest is foolishness."

Clarissa digested the words of the duchess. She felt something inside herself flicker. Maybe it was possible that she and David could be together. She realized that going from being the Duchess's companion to being a Duchess herself was still a major leap in status. She could not blend into the background, as she liked to do. She had never liked London, and always felt ill at ease in crowds, or as the center of attention. If she married David, she would be a Duchess, and she knew it would be expected that they spend part of the year in the city, while the House of Lords was in session, and that she attend, and even host events on a regular basis. She would be taking on a much bigger role than wife. Could she do that? Did she want to?

"I still have them, if you would like to see them." The Duchess said, interrupting her thoughts.

"You have what?"

"The letters, David wrote you, years ago. I still have them. I never opened them, I promise. If you would like to read them, they are yours," she offered.

"Where are they?"

"In my room, at the back of the bottom left drawer of my vanity, they are tied with a purple ribbon."

"May I retrieve them?"

"Certainly, my dear, they are yours, after all. I am only sorry I did not give them to you sooner."

Clarissa helped the Duchess back to bed. She then proceeded to the vanity, and opened the bottom left drawer. It was full of all manner of things. It took a few minutes to dig through the debris to the bottom back of the drawer to find the stack of letters. There had to be at least forty or fifty letters. All with David's familiar scrawl on the front and his wax Hollister seal on the back. She bid the Duchess goodnight and went to her room where she untied the ribbon, and picked up the first letter, and broke the seal. She sat down to read it.

My Dearest, Clarissa,

We have stopped at an Inn for the night. How I wish you were here with me. With each mile that passes, I regret more and more how we parted this morning. I wanted so badly to take you in my arms, and kiss you, love you, for I do love you, and I should have told you so, a hundred times. Please give me the chance to tell you in the future? I know I am young, and perhaps foolish, but I know that my feelings for you are true and forever.

My mother and I talked yesterday; as I'm sure she talked to you also. She said several things that I don't agree with, but she did say one thing, that if I did not have my title or wealth, I would have nothing to offer you. I would beg to differ, as I offer you my heart. Still, I realize that is not enough. For this reason, I did make the decision to go back to school. I have to finish this year at Eton, then on to Cambridge. I hope you understand leaving you was the most difficult thing I have ever done. I wish we could have parted on better terms. Even now, all I can think is jumping in the carriage and demanding they turn it around towards home, towards you. I hope to return to you, a better man than the one that left. If I have one goal, it is that.

I know you are in mourning for your mother, and

I regret that I cannot be there. More than anything, I wish I were. Please know that I am doing this for us, for our future. Education is a thing to be prized, isn't that what the Duchess always said? I hope that someday you will be proud of my achievements and that it will all be worth it.

With Eternal Love,
David.

Clarissa set the letter aside with shaking hands. How her sixteen-year-old self would have cherished this, she thought. Eight years later she was moved to tears. Right here was proof that he had loved her. Did he still? She wanted to believe it. She knew her feelings for him had not changed, but she was not a starry eyed girl, now. She had grown and changed, and so had David. Did they really even know each other, anymore?

She pulled a letter off the bottom of the stack. The date was September, several months later, and the return address was Cambridge. He'd come home for nearly a month, between leaving Eton and going to Cambridge. She had spent that month doing her level best to avoid him, retreating every time he came near, and outright hiding when she had to. He and the Duchess had been at odds, nearly every day during that stay, and he had left weeks earlier than expected. She had to wonder now how that time would have turned out so differently if she had received these letters. She also had to acknowledge how hurt David had been. Several times he had tried to talk to her, but she had turned away and refused to listen. If only she had not been so stubborn, or so afraid of being made a fool again. She had wronged him greatly, by letting her own doubts and insecurities get the better of her. She had driven him away.

She opened the last letter.

My Dearest, Clarissa

I have lain here; awake in my bed for hours, pondering what words I could say that would bring you back to me. In so many letters I have expressed my love and devotion to you, with no reply. I have to assume that it is all one sided, and that your feelings for me has changed, or in fact, never existed at all. I look back on our night together, so many months ago. I thought our passion was mutual, but in hindsight I wonder if you thought I was taking advantage of you in a moment of weakness. If that is your feeling, I offer my most sincere apology. I would rather take my own life than hurt you, Clary.

These last few weeks back at Hollister haunt me. I regret that now you feel you have to avoid me. The fact that you would not speak to me or even look me in the eye showed me how much I have wronged you. No words can express how I long to make things right again, but I confess, I do not know how. What can I say that I have not already said in dozens of letters?

What would make this right again? Please, Clary, tell me and I will do it.

I am leaving this in your hands now. If I have no reply, yet again, I will accept that your love for me is no more, and I promise I will not bother you again.

Yours, most sincerely,
David

Her heart constricted as she finished reading this letter. He had written several in between and she had replied to none of them. Clarissa wondered if there was any way now to completely mend the breach between them. She had hurt him greatly. No apology now would be grand enough to undo all the damage that had been done between them. She pondered going to him now. There was no doubt he would welcome her into his room, and into his bed. Would that really resolve anything? The desire was still there, but what of the trust, the respect, that, she'd have to earn back. With a sad sigh, setting the letters aside she readied for bed, slipping under the covers, never having felt so alone in her life.

Chapter Twenty-One

She was back to being cool towards him. He thought things had finally changed for them yesterday, that they had reached a point of understanding and acceptance.

Clary had been quiet last night, but today, as the hours went by he could tell that something was eating at her. She sat quietly while he and the Duchess went over business and talked of the various investments that would need attention. He tried hard to concentrate on all the information his mother was giving him, but it was difficult with Clarissa nearby, seemingly with a cloud over her head. Finally, his mother claimed fatigue and he took his leave so she could rest.

He waited in the hallway while Clarissa attended his mother. When she finally came out several minutes later, without a word he took her by the hand and led her down the stairs. At first she resisted, and tried to pull away but he quelled that with a lowering of his brow.

He led her into the library, and closed the

door. She gave him a glare, and shook off his hand, crossing her arms as she strode away from him towards the fireplace. She stared off into the low burning embers before she finally spoke, her voice low and inflexible.

"You know nothing of discretion. It does not bode well for me, to appear to be carrying on with the master of the house."

"Is that what this is about? You are embarrassed about what people might think? You think we should continue this affair in hiding?"

"Affair," she scoffed, "we are not in an affair, whatever is going on between us, and we do not need to draw attention to it."

"So you want to continue to ignore the feelings we have for each other? I thought yesterday we had settled that we were beyond that, at least."

"It was almost cruel, what you did yesterday, you should have dropped my hand or let go, as soon as you realized anyone else was around. I don't know why you didn't."

"Don't you? So I am not to acknowledge that I have any feelings for you? After what we shared earlier, I thought I had every right."

"It hurt Darius, not to mention Robbie. I know it did. I feel like you did it deliberately. Darius is a kind man, and I would never hurt him for the world."

"So I am not allowed to lay claim to you, to avoid the hurt of all the men who clearly have a tendre for the fair Miss Clarissa? My feelings are of no consequence?"

Clarissa turned away from him indignantly, and faced the fire. He could tell she was trying to reign in her temper. He wanted to apologize, he knew he'd had no right, and was reacting out of pure jealousy. It seemed to him that she was deliberately picking a fight to keep him at a distance. He would not have it.

She turned back to him, her shoulders thrown back and her bearing regal. He wasn't sure why, but he looked to the painting over her head, his parents wedding portrait. She stood so that she was just under it, centered between his mother and father. Her posture, her build, even the bone structure of her face was so like his mothers, the way she looked in the portrait. And the blue eyes and blond hair so like his father. He looked down at Clarissa, then up at the portrait again. His ears roared. It...couldn't be. No...he had to be imagining it. Surely, it wasn't possible...

"Are you listening to me?" her voice finally penetrated.

"What? I'm sorry...what did you say?" he asked

"I said that I am merely friends with Darius and Lucas, not to mention Reggie and Robbie, nothing more. I certainly have no romantic designs on any of them. Not that it is any of your business," she clarified, and then noted his shell shocked expression. "David, what's wrong?" she asked in alarm.

He opened his mouth to reply but then closed it. He dared not speak of this, at least not with Clarissa, not yet. He had to be wrong. It couldn't possibly be true.

"Pardon me...I need to speak with my mother, right now," he said backing out of the room. He was at a full sprint by the time he hit the stairs, and reaching his mother's suite. He stopped to catch his breath and try to regain his composure. Without knocking, he entered closing and locking the door behind him. His mother was lying in bed, a book in her hands, lamplight lit the room, and she put her book down.

"Darling, what is it?" she asked. He noted her voice was a bit more feeble than it had been earlier. Slowly he approached the bed, and sat down on the edge. He was afraid of looking a fool for the questions he needed to ask, but he was more afraid of the answers. He reached across the coverlet and took her hand in his. He looked into her eyes, and at once saw, that she knew...

"Mother, I...I was in the library with Clarissa just now. She was standing under the portrait of you and father, and I noticed...Mother, I must ask...I need to know...is Clarissa your daughter, did you give birth to her?" His heart beat like a drum in his chest, and as he waited, she swallowed and gathered her words. A sheen of tears came to her eyes.

"I promised, if you ever asked, I would tell you the truth. Yes, she is my daughter."

"Mother...is Clary my sister? Do we share blood?" he asked hoarsely.

"You are my son, but no, you do not share blood. She is not your sister." He wasn't prepared for the wave of relief that washed over him. He felt almost lightheaded. Thank God! If he had found out that they were related; he couldn't even bear thinking it. On the heels of that thought another question occurred. If she was not related to him, then who was?

"Who...how...?" He asked, stymied by the myriad of questions this knowledge now brought up.

"Annabelle birthed you. Please, David, know that in my heart you are my son. I love you. You have to understand, there were circumstances."

"So...Annabelle was my mother, and ...George was my father? The ladies' maid and the footmen were my real parents?" he asked incredulously. Springing to his feet, facing her, she shook her head, adamantly.

"You are MY son, Annabelle put you in my arms and gave your life to me, trusted your life to me. Everything I have is yours."

"What of Clary? How can you deny her? She is your blood, not I," he demanded to know.

"Annabelle loved her, you know she did, and I have loved her too. She has wanted for nothing."

He shook his head "But she is treated as a servant..."

"She is treated as a daughter, to the best of my ability. It hasn't been easy. But it was the only way. You have to understand," the Duchess insisted.

"Mother!" he said, still reeling in shock "My whole life is a lie. I'm not the Duke, I never was."

"You are the Duke! You were brought up to be one. Educated and presented as such. No good can come of denying it now," she stated emphatically.

"But...it's not true. I'm not the rightful heir, I never was."

"Sit down!" The duchess demanded. Reluctantly, he obeyed and retook his seat. She reached over and gently took his hand within both of her own, and took a deep breath, before she began to speak again, "When I met your father...Dorian, the estate was in ruins. Dorian was many things, but no business man. He had let his uncle, Lord Grey, run the estate which was a huge mistake, as he took it into great debt. Do you know Lord Grey actually convinced Dorian to pursue me for my dowry? But we did fall in love with each other, and we married. My one condition, that Lord Grey no longer has any say in the management of the estate, Dorian was more than happy to turn the running of it over to me. I have always had a head for business, from my father. As you can imagine, Lord Grey was not happy," she told him. "Shortly after we married, my father passed away. His title was left to a distant cousin, and some entailed properties. But the majority of his holdings were left to me, or since I was married, by law it was left to my husband. That didn't bother me, because we were partners and shared everything."

"Then he died."

"Yes, then he died. Along with your true father George. MacPherson was just a boy then; he saw the whole thing. George tried to fight them off, defending and protecting Dorian to the end. But, he was killed, and then so was Dorian. When we found out...that was the most horrible day of my life. Of Annabelle's too."

"Is that when you decided to switch us, if you didn't have a son?"

"No! You have to understand, we didn't go into this, with a plan at all. I hoped I would have a boy, but if I had a girl, I was resigned to my fate of losing everything. I truly was. Lord Grey came by on a weekly basis to see if I'd 'whelped' yet, as he liked to put it. He made it very clear that if the baby I birthed was a girl, he fully intended to take the property back and force me, and my child, not to mention the staff that was loyal to me, out."

"You told me that the day I was born, he showed up, and threatened me. Why did he think I was yours?"

"You were born early that morning to Annabelle, and the moment you were born, at your first cry actually, I felt my first pain of labor. I believe that Clarissa heard you through the womb and was demanding an introduction." She smiled wryly.

He had to smile, too. Clarissa was never known for her patience.

"I gave birth late that night, to her. She was very small; not much more than half the size you were. At first she didn't cry-I was so frightened; the longest minute of my life was waiting for her to cry when she was birthed. I loved her at first sight, but she was so fragile and delicate. She terrified me, you both did. Annabelle was with me the whole time, despite her own exhaustion.

"We heard Lord Grey. He was...drunk, and frightening. As he stomped up the stairs, all I could think was that I had to hide her, protect her from him. I had just given birth not two hours before. That was the only thought in my head. Without a word, Annabelle took Clarissa and climbed into the wardrobe and shut the door.

"Do you know I didn't even realize that she had left you behind in the cradle, until he was already in the room? I was horrified when he went for you. I had to stop him. I jumped out of the bed but he knocked me down. I grabbed the fireplace poker, and when I saw him raise his hand to you... I hit him, with more strength than I thought I had in me. I don't even remember what I said, but I told him to get out and never come near me or my child again. Then Franklin showed up, with all the footmen in tow and they drug him out of here. He left, thinking I had given birth to a boy."

"And you never corrected him."

"Annabelle made the decision, for us. She placed you in my arms; she gave you to me, to be my son. To become the Duke, to protect us all, but in turn, I...had to give up my Clarissa." She said, a tear spilling from her eye.

"I don't know what to think. Mother...I'm not even sure I should call you that anymore."

"Of course you should. My darling David, you did not come from my body, but I was there when you drew your first breath. Your birth mother, Annabelle, was my closest, most trusted friend whom I loved dearly. Had she not given you to me, I would have still loved you. But she did, and I could only love you more, even though it broke my heart to deny Clarissa as my daughter, too."

"Oh God...Clary, I don't know...how can I face her now? Just knowing what my presence has denied her?"

"David...Clarissa knows. We told her, Annabelle told her, shortly before she died."

"She's known? All this time," he was stunned, disbelieving. He stood up and instinctively took a step back from the bed. She knew, Clary never said a word to him. She was the one person he had thought that he could trust over anyone else, his soul mate, and his confidant. But she had kept this from him. He felt a fool. What must she have thought, when he was going off to Eton and Cambridge, when he was mixing with the ton in London, while she was exiled to the estate, at the beck and call of the Duchess? Why did she never tell him? He felt so many things. Sad, confused, angry, but the emotion he felt above all else was betrayal. He could almost understand his mother keeping this a secret, but Clarissa? She had let him live a lie, for years. Let herself be diminished by that lie. That was what angered him the most.

"Thank you for being honest with me, Mother. I need...I need to think," he said. She nodded, sadly.

But, I'm not sorry that I got to be your Mother. You are a truly good man, and it has been my... privilege to call you my son. Don't ever think otherwise," she told him. He felt tears come to his eyes, and a lump in his throat. He could only nod to acknowledge her words, and then left the room, shutting the door quietly behind him.

In the hallway, stood Clarissa, she had her arms crossed defensively; her eyes were huge in her face. "She told you," she guessed.

"I figured it out. She confirmed it. She told me you've known since before Annabelle died. How...God Clary, all this time, and you've never said a word? I don't understand how you could keep this from me? How you must hate me?" he whispered in anguish.

She shook her head and stepped forward. She took his hand in hers, and without a word, led him down the hall, to her room. He let her pull him inside, shutting the door.

"I don't hate you. I hope you can forgive me, forgive the Duchess and Annabelle."

"Clary...my whole life, it's a huge lie. I'm not a Duke; I'm the footman's son. All this time, I thought I could not have you because of our stations. The harsh truth is that it is I who was never worthy of you. You're a Lady, and I am...nothing!"

"Davey! You're everything! It hasn't all been a lie," she whispered. She took his hand and placed it over her heart. "This has always been true. My heart has always been yours. I don't care if you're a Duke or a pauper. I never have. I have tried to hold you at a distance, to protect you, to protect this secret our mothers entrusted to me," she said, tears spilling over and clogging her throat. "I can't do it anymore. Whatever happens, I just need to be with you, whoever you are, wherever you are," she promised.

"Clary...my sweet girl, don't cry," he said, kissing her eyelids, following the trail of tears down her cheek, to the edge of her mouth. She turned into his lips, and opened to him. With a shuddering breath she melted against him.

"I need you...please Davey, love me," she

gasped against his mouth.

"God help me, I do. I always have." He picked her up and walked the few steps to the bed and laid her down on the mattress. He reached up and without breaking her gaze; he undid his cravat and tossed it aside, then unbuttoned his shirt and took it off. She untied the tie at the bottom of her corset and loosened it. She knelt up on the bed and took it off, and pulled her dress over her head along with her shift. His eyes drank in the sight of her alabaster breasts with their pink tipped nipples. He reached out and traced one with his finger, feeling it tighten against his touch.

He knelt on the bed and bent his head to take the tip between his lips. She gasped, and arched against him. Her fingers dug into his curls, and she cried out as he switched breasts and suckled the other nipple, nipping it lightly with his teeth. He pushed her back against the bed and braced himself over her as he stroked her with his fingers and lips and tongue.

He parted her legs and kissed his way down her belly. She still wore her garters and pantaloons. He untied the bow at her waist and loosened the pantaloons and drew them down her legs, undoing her garters, and sensually rolling down her stockings. Finally, she was completely bare. For a long moment he stared at her in awe, then realizing he was still mostly clothed. He quickly unbuttoned the placket to his breeches, releasing the strain against his groin, and turned as he sat on the edge of the bed, yanking off his boots and along with them, his dungarees and small clothes.

Crawling back to her he nudged her legs apart. He resumed where he had left off, kissing and licking his way down her belly, to the nest of blond curls at the apex of her thighs. Giving her a wicked smile, he bent down further and delved his tongue in her folds. Her hips came up off the bed. She grasped his head with her hands, when he found that hardened nub with the tip of his tongue she bucked against his mouth. He pulled closer to him. "Be still, I want to taste your pleasure, Clary." He breathed.

"Davey...oh God...I need...I need..."

"Come on Clary, I want it all." He demanded and redoubled his efforts, his tongue and lips working her. With one hand he delved into her depths, plunging one finger into her wet tightness, then two. The tips of his fingers bumped up against her innocence and he felt immeasurably humbled that he was the only man to love her like this. God willing, the only man who ever would. He was rewarded with her whole body quaking and shuddering and her juices flooded his hand, his mouth. He lapped and licked until the last shiver stopped. He levered himself over her. "This is going to hurt...I'm sorry. But after that, is pleasure. I promise." He whispered. She nodded, and reached up and framed his face within her delicate hands, and leaned up to kiss him, reveling in the taste of herself on his lips.

"I trust you. Please...I need you inside me." She begged. His cock probed at her entrance and then worked its way inside her. She was so tight, so hot and wet. He wanted nothing more than to plunder her, but he strained to take it slowly, until he was bumping up against her barrier. He bent his head and kissed her deeply as he drew back, then plunged forward. She arched and cried out in pain, against his mouth. He held himself still, until he felt her relax and then began to gently glide in and out. He kissed her forehead, sweetly.

"You're mine, now." He said.

"I always was." She smiled, wrapping her thighs around him and arching her hips against his, encouraging his possession.

He took her deeper and quickened his pace. Taking both of her hands in his, he braced them above her head and started thrusting in earnest. She raised her hips each time to meet his and cried out, looking into his eyes as she reached the summit again. "Davey!" She cried in wonder, spasming around him.

He let go and spent deeply inside her, collapsing atop her, with a guttural moan, burying his face against her neck. She wrapped her arms around him, sighing deeply, rolling to his side, pulling her into the cradle of his embrace.

"I have dreamed of this. I had nearly given up believing that it would ever come to be." He said, pulling back so that he was looking her in the eye.

"I think that it was inevitable." She said, lazily tracing a finger over the contours of his chest.

"Clary...I love you, I want to marry you. But I want you to know...I have not resolved what to do with the Dukedom. I can't with good conscious, take it up knowing now that I was never the one born to it. Still, to give it up is to take it away from you, too. We are in a precarious position right now, you and I. Can you give me your troth, even knowing this?"

"My Darling Davey...if you were a king or a beggar, my love for you would be the same. I love you for your heart, and your mind, not for your title or your holdings. This was the legacy their secret bought us."

"In truth...they are your title and holdings. How can you not resent me, having what you so richly deserve?"

"I will tell you something. When I was a girl, one time my mother-Annabelle asked me if I ever wished I were the daughter of the Duchess. I was horrified, at that time, because though I loved the Duchess, Annabelle was my mother, in my heart, she always was. When she was dying...she told me the truth and I realized that I had been so lucky, to have had her, to ground me and guide me. If I had been acknowledged as the daughter of the Duke and the Duchess from birth, how horrid would I have been?"

"As horrid as me?" he said and she playfully slapped him on the arm.

"I would not say that! It is different for the male heirs, as you know. You have a purpose, a mission. The female offspring are but decorative bargaining tools. I am glad that was not my fate. I feel that I was fated to be with you, and this is the only way it could have happened."

"Then I should be happy about our mothers' deception?"

"You will have to decide for yourself if that is something you can live with. I can assure you it was not done with malice. Our mothers were in a desperate situation and did what they felt they had to do to protect us and themselves. Whether it was right or wrong, I cannot say."

"You do know that this means that Lord Grey is justified in his actions, that he should have been the rightful Duke on the death of my-your father."

"Not if he is the one responsible for his death."

"We do not know for sure that he was. We only have the Duchess's feelings on the matter, but there is no actual proof. We do not even know for certain that he was the one behind the attack on our carriage. We are just assuming it is all him, because he is the one with the most to gain."

"Who else would do this? Have you accumulated any great enemies among the ton?"

"Well…no. Perhaps a few fellows I've won sums off, when gambling. But no one who would wish to see me harmed."

"No angry husbands would be coming after you?"

"Clary…I have never been with a married woman. I would never do that. Truth is told I haven't been with anyone in over a year. I just… you have always been the only woman I've ever wanted. Anyone else was but a poor substitute."

"I believe you. I think all this time, whether I admitted it or not, I've been waiting for you to come back. I have wanted no other."

"I believe you, too."

"So no more jealousy?"

"Was I really that obvious?"

"Yes, but I'm glad. At least I knew you still had feelings for me."

"That will never change."

"So what will we do now?"

"I want to marry you. Will you have me Clary?" He asked.

"Of course, have I not said I am yours? My only concession is that I want the Duchess there, so our wedding must be soon."

"If you are insistent on marrying quickly, I need to get a special license from the Archbishop. He is in London, right now, so I need to go there. If I go on horseback and leave at dawn, I can be back in two days' time."

"I feel I must stay with the Duchess, but please do not go alone. Take Lucas and Darius with you for protection."

"I do not want to leave you unprotected here."

"All the men of the house have been trained. I think we will be fine; I am more worried about you. Promise me you will take them with you."

"If you insist, I will make that request of them. I promise."

"Thank you. Now, before you go, maybe you should give me another sample of what I can expect of marital relations," she said wickedly.

"Gladly," he said, kissing her shoulder. He drew the sheet down her body and followed the path with his mouth. Kissing and suckling her breasts, until she arched against him. Open mouthed kisses along her belly and hip. She splayed herself open to his gaze and he thought no sight was more erotic.

He settled himself between her hips and teased her with his hardness. She thrust up, trying to impale herself on him but he held back, teasing her still. Finally, finally he slid home, into her warmth and they both sighed in satisfaction. She clutched her thighs about his and locked her ankles behind his back, holding him deep within her.

He began to move, slowly rocking into her. Unlike last time, this time he drew out the pleasure of every moment, building the passion slowly, taking her deeper, until he could not tell where he ended and she began.

In this moment he truly felt that they were one, that the two of them made a whole that could never be broken. He looked into her face and was awed by the love in her eyes, the passion, all for him. He felt something in him expand. He knew if he lived to be a hundred, this was how he would always remember her. Beautiful, passionate, as they reached the apex of their pleasure they both kept their eyes open, watching each other and it was an arc that seemed to go back and forth between them endlessly. His seed filled her, and could feel a sensation, like life was being created. He sincerely hoped it was true.

Chapter Twenty-Two

Clarissa opened the curtains then crossed the room to the Duchess's bed. She was so frail, and had no more color than the sheets around her. For a moment she feared the worst, then Drusilla's eyes fluttered open, and a soft smile came to her face. "Good morning, my darling." The Duchess said. Clarissa sat down at the side of her bed, and took her hand.

"Good morning, Your Grace. How are you feeling today?"

"I awoke to your beautiful face, so I feel happy." She said simply. "David came to see me last night. I told him everything."

"I know. He told me. He and I spoke," Clarissa told her, and help but blush, thinking of all the other things they had done.

"Why do I have a feeling, there was more than just talking?" The Duchess insinuated.

Clarissa wasn't sure how to say what she needed to say, she didn't want to upset the Duchess, but it was also important that she had her love and approval. "David asked me to marry him." Clarissa watched Drusilla's face for any trace of anger, but instead she saw a resigned, knowing expression.

"Do you love him?"

"I do. Very much, I always have," Clarissa admitted. The Duchess nodded, smiling softly.

"Do you know, when you were infants, you were both so fretful when you were apart. We would put you in the same cradle, and as soon as you were together, you would both calm. I think I knew even then, there was no stopping this. You two have always needed each other."

"You aren't angry?"

"I've had much time to reflect, especially these last few months. I have realized that the one thing I want most, have always wanted, was for you, and for David to be happy. You make each other happy. I can no longer stand in the way of that. I should never have tried."

"Thank you, Your Grace...do you think...do you think Mama would be pleased?"

"I believe Annabelle saw this coming, long before I did. I remember once we were watching you playing when you were children and she said "Look at them, look how they light up when they are together. I think that is the light of love." And she was right. I know that for a time I was so worried about the legacy of the Duchy and also worried that the secret would come out and destroy us all...but I know that no matter what happens, you will weather it together."

"David has gone to get a special license. We wish to marry right away, and want you to be there."

"I would be most proud. If you would...there is a white painted chest in the attic. Can you ask the footmen to retrieve it and bring it here?"

"Yes, yes of course." Clarissa attended to the task. Returning several minutes later, followed by two footmen carrying the chest. They placed it next to the bed. At Drusilla's behest, Clarissa opened the chest to see the pale blue gown that Drusilla had worn in her wedding portrait. She carefully pulled it out; it was scented of roses and cedar and had been neatly wrapped in muslin. Beneath the gown was a fine lace veil, the likes of which she had never seen.

"Oh, Your Grace, it is so beautiful, I don't know what to say," Clarissa breathed.

"I had always hoped to see my daughter in that dress. I know it may not be the style now, but I was a very happy bride in that dress. I want you to have it."

"I am overwhelmed..." Clarissa said, unable to stop tears from coursing down her face. She crawled up on the bed and embraced the duchess. She cried in joy, which quickly turned to sorrow. What would she do when she was gone? Was it fair to have to lose not one, but two mothers in a lifetime? The Duchess caressed her hair and held her in her frail arms, and let her cry. As the tears were winding down, a knock on the bedroom door interrupted them.

"Ladies, may I come in?" It was the doctor, Reginald. Clarissa gathered herself together quickly, and got off the bed, and blew her nose in her handkerchief.

"Of course, come in Reggie. I'm sorry; we were having a bit of a maudlin moment." Clarissa explained.

"Congratulations are in order, Reginald. Our Clarissa and His Grace are going to be married." The Duchess announced. Reginald looked to Clarissa and searched her face then offered a stilted smile.

"My best wishes to you and His Grace, Miss Clarissa. I am most happy for you," he said with a bow of his head.

"Thank you, Reggie. I am quite happy, too. David left for London early this morning, to get a special license. We will be married in three days' time. I would love it if you would come."

"I'd be honored, Miss Clarissa," he said, although it was evident that there was disappointment in his eyes.

David had told her once that the doctor had designs on her, although he had acted a complete gentleman the entire time she had known him. She sincerely hoped he was not truly hurt by her decision, as she knew what it was like to love someone you thought you could never have.

The doctor turned towards the Duchess. "Now, how about you, Duchess, how are you feeling this day?"

"Peaceful, Reggie, I unburdened myself to my son last night, and I feel like a weight has been lifted." Clarissa turned to the Duchess in surprise; she hadn't expected her to tell anyone else the truth of their parentage. The physician didn't seem surprised at all by the revelation. He glanced at Clarissa.

"So I suppose that you know, as well, that you are related to the Duchess?" Carissa's mouth fell open in shock. She looked between Reginald and the Duchess.

"You know? You told him?"

"When he mentioned the fact that this disease might be hereditary, I felt it necessary to let him know that you are my daughter, so that he could keep a close eye on your health." The Duchess explained.

"Then you know, that David..."

"Is not blood related to the late Duke or Her Grace, but their son, just the same? Yes." Reginald clarified. "It goes without saying; I will always keep this information in the strictest confidence."

"I...thank you Reggie. You are a true friend," Clarissa said gratefully. She had to wonder how long he had known, but decided it was not her place to ask. He would not have betrayed the Duchess's confidence without knowing that David, and she now knew the truth, and she could trust he would never tell anyone else. Whatever David decided to do regarding the title, she felt assured that David and she would be protected either way.

"Now, Doctor, it is a beautiful day, I think I would like to spend a few hours among my roses. Do you have any objections?" The Duchess decreed. Reginald smiled at her.

"I'm sure the fresh air would do you well, Your Grace." He nodded. "I'd be delighted to join you myself."

"Lovely. Clarissa, call for the footmen, we're going to the garden."

"Yes, Your Grace." She said, ringing for the footmen.

Chapter Twenty-Three

Lord Grey sat astride his horse on the edge of the woods and peered through his spyglass. He could see her, sitting in the garden, blankets wrapped about her, a wide brimmed hat on her head. He'd watched as the footmen had carried her out and placed her on the wicker lounge chair, lifting her as easily as a child. A young man had accompanied her for nearly an hour, regretfully, not the Duke, as well as a young blond woman.

He'd been camped in the woods for the last few nights, watching the house. He'd seen the Duke and the blonde walked into the trees opposite him just a few days before, but he'd been so far behind them, he'd lost them. They had emerged a few hours later and appeared to have an altercation, which then took a surprisingly passionate turn. That told him that the blonde maid meant something to the Duke. He wondered if he could use that to his advantage.

His attention returned to the Duchess. She had

the over thin appearance of an invalid unable to walk of her own accord. Even from this distance he could see the distinct gray pallor to her skin. So, he thought, MacPherson had lied. She was not getting better. Judging by the look of her, she likely had little time left. He expected to feel elation at the thought that Drusilla would soon be dead. Curiously, he felt nothing at all. How strange? For years he had dreamed of the day he would get what was rightfully his, biding his time. Waiting, still, a part of him wondered how things might have been if they had gone as planned, the first time.

His mind traveled back to the day Barstow Thoroughgood had died. Barstow was his nephew, although the man had been half a dozen years older than himself. He was a pompous prick of a man who had loved to bully him as a child, always making disparaging remarks about Grey's mother, a woman he did not even remember, she, having left on the death of her elderly husband when it was apparent he had left little provision for her in his will, abandoning an infant Grey to the care of his half-brother, the Eighth Duke of Hollister.

He'd been raised alongside his nephews, the older Barstow and slightly younger Dorian. It had always been obvious that they were the welcome and beloved children in the family, and he, Grey, merely an interloper they were saddled with.

Barstow had been horrid to him. Dorian...he had been kind, treating him as a brother. However, Dorian had only want of being a soldier, had left home at the first opportunity to join the ranks, leaving him alone with Barstow, who had ordered him about like a servant for his own amusement.

He'd never forget the day he had been ordered to go riding with Barstow, who was by then, the Ninth Duke of Hollister. He'd seen the snake on their path, but it was clear that Barstow had not. To this day, he did not know why he had not warned him, or why he held his own horse back and let Barstow's horse go forth, without a word.

Why, when the horse reared in fear he did not immediately go to Barstow's aid and help him get the horse under control. Or why, he merely watched as the horse bucked and threw Barstow like a rag doll, against the heavy rocks strewn about the path. Why, instead of going for help, he merely sat on his own horse, for what seemed like hours while Barstow's blood soaked the dirt around him, until it stopped flowing entirely.

Why he felt no regret.

Weeks later, when Dorian had returned home, after resigning his military commission to take his place as the Tenth Duke of Hollister, he'd offered his assistance. Dorian, though a fine soldier, had been clearly out of his depth as Duke, a title he had never expected to hold. Grey had offered his services, and Dorian had been happy to accept, letting Grey take care of everything, without question. They'd muddled through peacefully for a few years, but soon the money was gone, and Grey had to make a plan.

Grey had met Lady Drusilla at a London ball. She was the daughter of the wealthiest shipping magnate of the country, a newly appointed Earl, and a personal friend of Prinny.

Lady Drusilla was in her fourth season, and her father had doubled her dowry. Not because she wasn't beautiful. She was quite striking with flashing green eyes, and luxuriant red hair she wore, in a crown of curls about her head. But she was particularly headstrong, and ambitious in her own right, and refused all suits. No one had been good enough for her hand.

Grey had wanted her on sight. They'd danced and talked and he had wanted to make her his. She had boldly flirted with him, he sensed she was not above a dalliance with him but had set her sights higher. He saw in her an opportunity, the chance to have it all if he could entice her to play along.

He told her of his nephew, a war hero, who on the recent demise of his older brother, now held the title of Duke of Hollister, and must carry on the family line. Dorian, who had never expected to be the Duke, had no head for business and no interest in running the estate. He bragged how, despite his nephew holding the title, it was he, Grey, who held the power.

He did not tell her that the family fortune was nearly gone, that he had gambled away most of it. At first he thought to woo Lady Drusilla himself. Lord Grey knew that Drusilla's dowry alone would see him well, the remainder of his days, not to mention the fact that her father was in ill health and intended to leave his fortune to his only child. When it was evident that she thought his own rank of Baron, not high enough for her liking, he changed tactics. He pointed out that his nephew the Duke would need to marry and provide an heir. He took advantage of the fact that her father was in ill health, and desperate for her to make a match. The father's fortune would go to the husband of the Lady Drusilla, as well. He could just picture it, all that money, the extravagances he could have with that. He, Lord Grey, would control it all, and once Drusilla had done her duty, she would be his for the taking.

Unlike himself, Dorian hated going to London. Preferring instead to spend his days tramping about on horseback around Brookshire, with his friend George, who had been his batman when he was in the military, at his side. George's official capacity was head footman, although he was more of a bodyguard to Dorian, than anything. Lord Grey hated George, for he was a shrewd man and had an uncanny way of looking at him, as if he could see his deepest darkest secrets.

The house party had been his idea, he had arranged the whole thing, he had confided in Drusilla all of Dorian's likes and dislikes, and had invited a number of other ladies, all much less desirable than Drusilla, to give her the edge. He knew Dorian, was gullible in the face of a beautiful woman, and knew Drusilla would make a practical choice and accept Dorian's hand, when asked. He was certain she would reward him mightily for arranging the match.

He had planned it all so well, or so he thought, at the time, but didn't factor in that Drusilla would actually fall in love with Dorian. He hadn't imagined that she'd take an interest in the running of Hollister herself, or that she'd go over the books so carefully and then go to her husband and point out all the grievous things he had done, the way he had robbed the estate and decreased its value while Dorian let him have control.

He had not been prepared for Dorian to cast him aside, his own flesh and blood, in favor of his new bride and for him to happily turn over the running of all of his holdings over to her. When her father died a few months into the marriage, his financial holdings had all gone to his son in law, Dorian, as husband to his only child. The estate was now a hundred times worth the amount as it had been before. The only thing standing between it and him and all that wealth were Dorian and Drusilla. If they died without progeny, he would be the Duke. When he heard that Drusilla was with child, he began to make his plan.

By then, he had been banned from the estate but he still had MacPherson, his own informant on the inside. He had lifted the child out of squalor and he seemed quite happy to report every little detail back to him. When the young MacPherson told him the Dorian and Drusilla had intended a trip to Tattersalls, to purchase more horses for their stable, he knew the opportunity he had been seeking had presented itself.

He had hired the men, and had even gone with them to assure that the couple would be killed. He imagined standing over them as they drew their last breath, and the thought had given him untold joy. When the carriage had rounded the bend where they waited, he had been so excited. He'd hung back as all hell had broken loose. He'd been most upset to find that Drusilla had not been with Dorian that day, after all. His only consolation was that George, who had been a pain in his side for years, died a bloody death, as he tried to shield Dorian from the hail of gunfire that came at them. When Grey emerged from his hiding spot, he was disappointed to find them both already dead, and felt a bit thwarted that they he never got that moment to stand over them in his glory.

He paid off the bandits, delivered a dire warning to young MacPherson, and gone home, and waited.

When he received word the next day that Dorian was dead he had gone straight to Drusilla to offer consolation.

She refused to receive him.

He called again the next day, and again, she refused. He sent her a very kindly worded letter with his condolences, and offered to take care of the funeral arrangements and give his assistance with running the estate. Her reply had been terse and rather rude, he thought, denying any need of his assistance and requesting he leave her alone in her grief.

He'd curled up that note in his hand and grown more and more incensed. How dare she! He had all but handed her the title of Duchess. She had turned his nephew against him, then refused any offer he had made of politeness, would not even receive him. She had pushed him aside, even though by all rights he was now the rightful heir.

After some days ruminating on this, and drinking to excess, he went back to Hollister House. When the butler gave her regrets, yet again, he pushed past the man and went from room to room until he found her in the library. There she was with her ladies' maid. Regrettably he had lost control. He had shouted at her, and told her he was forcing her out of Hollister, as he was the rightful heir, now. Had she not shunned him so, he would have allowed her to stay, and warm his bed, now he would have her out on the street.

He had expected her to cower and beg to stay.

He had not expected her to summon every able bodied man in the household and have him bodily removed.

The next day he received the first of many home calls from her solicitor, informing him that until she gave birth, he had no right to Hollister House or any of the assets of the Hollister Duchy. So he waited.

He had ensured that the moment she gave birth; MacPherson would come to him directly to deliver the news. Unfortunately, the stupid boy forgot to ask if the newborn infant was male or female before setting out, so he had gone himself, to find out.

He had convinced himself that she would have a girl. He was so certain, so certain that he would be able to simply cast her and the babe out that very night. He had envisioned her, begging him to stay, to reconsider. But he had no use for Dorian's used goods. He would be Duke. He had been drinking that night of course, and much of his ire was fueled by whiskey.

He had pushed the men aside that would keep him away from Drusilla. He remembered running up the stairs to her chambers, the men on his heels, and into her room, locking the door behind himself to keep them out. The newborn babe was in the cradle next to her bed. She had tried to stop him, but he merely pushed her aside, he had to know, had to see.

When he unswaddled the babe and realized it was a boy, all the vile emotion rose in him like a red haze, and the only thought that penetrated to the forefront of his crazed, drunken mind, was to rid the world of this thing that thwarted all of his dreams. Before he could land the killing blow, Drusilla had cracked a mighty strike to his forearm with a fire poker, breaking the bone. The rest was a painful blur as she threatened him and her staff escorted him out into the rainy night.

Her solicitor visited him again the next day and laid out what was to be the cursed course of his life. He was to stay no less than fifty miles away from the Hollister House at all times, and never to approach the child, or Drusilla. In return, he was given a home near the border of Scotland, and a small staff, that was loyal to the person paying them, Drusilla. His quarterly allowance was just enough to keep him in food and ale and no more.

Defeated, he retreated to the hated estate in the middle of nowhere.

For years he wallowed in misery, reliving the mistakes that had brought him to this place, resenting all that he could have had, had things gone as planned. Then, as time went by he began to imagine what would happen if the boy died.

With no other heir, it would all come to him. He sent a few of his precious coins to MacPherson every month, to ensure that the boy kept him informed of the news of the Duchy. Most of those letters were clearly worthless, and said nothing of any great importance. Mainly that the boy Duke rarely left the estate and was rarely away from his mother.

Then a letter had come with news he could use. When he found out that the boy was going to Eton, he had seen his chance, and gone, waiting, thinking somehow away from his mother's watchful eye, some "mishap" might occur. He thought he had been careful, but Drusilla had seen him nosing around the grounds. Had set the guards on him and had him driven out of town. She'd even assigned a bodyguard to the boy, and as punishment had refused his quarterly stipend, leaving him with no funds at all for months.

It had taken him over a decade to save the bit he needed to pay off the hooligans to kill David this time, and still they bungled the job, leaving him now in a position to have to do it himself. Luckily he had found a number of men who had no scruples and were apparently more than happy to do his bidding for the coin he offered. He'd gathered six men, all armed to the teeth, and ready to strike at a moment's notice. He would just need to wait for that perfect moment to arrive.

Chapter Twenty-Four

It was a three hours since the sun had slipped below the horizon. The moon was full, and the only light that brightened their path. They were less than five miles from the estate, and had been in the saddle since early morning.

Lucas and Darius had been great companions during this trip. When he had knocked on their door before dawn the day prior, and asked them to accompany him as his protection, they had not hesitated. David had left Robbie behind to mind their livestock while they were gone, and the three of them had ridden straight through to London, spending the hours deep in conversation. As he had already agreed to finance their venture, in return for their protection, he had been glad of the opportunity to learn more about their plans.

They had readily answered his questions, and with a bit of prompting, had admitted that they both saw the distillery as the beginning of a much bigger venture. The brothers were ambitious and intelligent, and despite their afflictions, hard working. David could not help but be swept up in their enthusiasm and promised his support in financing and resources to their venture. He had no doubt it would be a solid investment that would pay him back many times over in its returns.

They had arrived in London past midnight, the day before and stayed the night at his townhouse. He had been relieved to see that his friend Kenton Fairchild, had taken him at his word, and moved in-and with him had come staff. The place was much cleaner than he had left it, and he was grateful.

He had been surprised the night before, to be met by Kenton's sister, Lady Olivia, in her dressing gown on their arrival. She thought it was her brother coming back from a night at the club and had been shocked to see the Duke, and his two comrades walking in the door. She had handled the situation with grace and aplomb and ordered food and brandy and baths for them.

David was still amused, remembering the episode. Lucas, upon seeing Lady Olivia had gone from a grizzled, plain speaking, hardened war veteran, to a gentleman of the highest order. Executing a bow that was worthy of royalty, at her introduction.

David still wasn't sure why the recently widowed Lady Olivia was staying there, as it had been Kenton's greatest desire to have a place, away from his sisters-hence his staying at the townhouse while David was away at the estate. Sadly, he hadn't even had a chance to see his friend while he was there. At dawn he was off to the Archbishop to get the special license, and then they left London straight away.

Like the day before, they rode straight through. It would probably be near midnight by the time they arrived at the estate. Lucas and Darius had not complained once of the long tiresome trip, for that, he was grateful. Their hour's long conversation about their plans for the beer distillery had wound down, considerably. Now each man seemed content to ride in silent reflection, along the moonlit road.

He was anxious to get home, to see Clarissa. He patted the left side of the jacket he wore, for about the hundredth time since he'd left that morning, reassured that the special license he had ridden all the way to London, and back for, was still there. Tomorrow afternoon, he would marry her. He could picture a ceremony in his mother's rose garden, and imagine exchanging vows, the smile on Clarissa's face, when he finally made her his in the eyes of God and England.

He still could not believe, after all these years, he and Clarissa would finally marry. She knew he wasn't really a Duke. Knew that their future was precarious at best, but loved him enough to want to marry him anyway. He was almost glad of the darkness which hid what he was sure was a love-besotted grin on his face.

They were rounding a bend in the road that was hidden by a copse of trees. His horse's ears flickered and the animal took a hesitant side step, showing its anxiety. He glanced towards Lucas on his right, lifting his eyebrows quizzically. Lucas held his hand out in a fist in front of him, signaling them all to stop. Darius, who had been behind him, now came up on his left, as he carefully reached for his pistol where he had stashed it on top of his saddlebag. David also went for a weapon; a dagger he had sequestered in his boot. He had a pistol also, at the small of his back, tucked in his trousers under his jacket. He knew he could grab it quickly if things went badly. He prayed he was wrong.

Suddenly he felt a jarring, sharp pain in his shoulder as someone landed on top of him. He had been looking ahead and had not been at all prepared for someone to leap on top of him from the tree bow overhanging the path.

Lucas and Darius were just as startled as they wheeled around on their horses. Both of them drawing their guns, pointing them at the man on top of him, but it was obvious neither could get a clean shot.

He gripped the dagger, shoving it as hard as he could over his shoulder into the man's arm.

The man yowled, seemingly grasping for something on his back and the next thing he felt was a piercing, unbearable pain just below his shoulder blade.

With cold dread he realized the assailant must have plunged a blade into when he leapt from the tree. and was now doing his best to skewer him again with it. Gritting his teeth, he pulled his own dagger, out of the man's side then stabbed at him again. Finally, the culprit fell to the ground.

Not wanting to wait for other bandits to show up, and finish the job, the trio took off, galloping away. Each movement was agony, but necessary. They had ridden about two miles when he could take it no more and cried out for them to stop. Bent over the horse in pain he could say nothing else. Lucas jumped off his horse and came to him.

"Bloody Hell! Your Grace, you have a knife sticking out of your back!"

"Take it out," he ordered through gritted teeth.

Lucas hesitated, but was reaching for the blade when Darius stopped him. "No! Wait, he might bleed to death if we pull it out. We need a doctor. Dr. Bishop's house is but a few miles from here. We are probably little more than a mile from the estate. You take him to the estate and I will go retrieve the doctor." Darius offered.

"No-the vicar. Get the vicar!" David cried out.

"Your Grace now is not the time to be making confessions." Lucas reasoned.

"No...I need to marry Clarissa...if I die...she may be with child. I need to protect her. The vicar! Get him!" he begged. Darius looked to his brother.

"Get them both!" Lucas directed. "I'll get him to the estate, you go get them and bring them back quickly." Darius nodded, took off at a run. Lucas turned back to him.

"Your Grace, we can't stay out here...there may be others. Can you hold on to your saddle if I take your reins and lead your horse?"

David nodded grimly. Lucas took his horses reins and then retook his own saddle. They set off at a bone jarring walk. David bent over the torso of his horse, the knife still sticking out of his back. Each movement was a new agony. He felt black spots in front of his eyes and he fought to focus. Clarissa. He had to stay alive long enough to marry her. He could do that. He would do that. But if he didn't...

"Lucas..." he called out.

"Do we need to stop, Your Grace?"

"No...keep going. I...need you to tell Clary, I loved her. I always loved her. I'm sorry I wasted so much time..."

"Your Grace, you can tell her yourself, we are almost there. See in the distance is the gate to the estate. She's there; Miss Clarissa is waiting for you. She needs you," Lucas pointed out.

David struggled to focus, but the blackness

was encroaching. The urge to give into it was strong. He felt himself losing consciousness. Just as he felt himself slipping away he felt a sharp sting to his cheek and he jerked back, awake. He held his hand to his stinging cheek and eyed Lucas, and saw a riding crop in his hand.

"Did you just hit me with a riding crop across the face?" he asked incredulously.

"Aye and I'll do it again, you damn bastard if it'll keep you from dying or falling off your horse. Now let's move!" Lucas ordered.

In all his life, as the Duke of Hollister, no one had ever spoken to him so forcefully, well, except for his own mother. He had to respect a man who would. David hesitated and Lucas raised the riding crop again.

"I'm awake! Bloody hell!"

They continued on, David clenched his jaw against the continuous pain. Finally, they arrived at the front door. Lucas dismounted and ran to pound on the door. Within moments a footman and Franklin were there, and between them and Lucas they carefully got him off of the horse and carried him inside.

He was taken to a parlor settee just off the foyer. He thought briefly that his mother would be quite upset to see blood stains on the upholstery.

"Clarissa." He breathed, aware of other people coming into the room. He could feel his jacket and shirt being cut away, and carefully pulled off of him. "The license, in the pocket, don't lose it," he insisted to the invisible hands helping him, and then he heard her.

"Davey!! What happened?" she cried, dropping to her knees beside him and grasping his hand.

"Clary, I'm fine," he insisted

"You are not fine! There is a knife in your back! Literally, that is the definition of not fine!"

"I made it though. I have the license. You must marry me the moment the vicar gets here."

"I'll do no such thing! You need a doctor..." he grabbed her hand

"Clary...it may already be too late to save me. If you are carrying my child, you need to marry me or he will take it all," he rasped.

"Don't say that! I don't want any of it, not without you!"

"I can't leave you with nothing."

"I...alright. I will marry you, but you have to promise to live. Will you promise me?" she asked. He nodded, even realizing he might be dying.

He could hear a commotion by the front door, and heard Dr. Bishop, the vicar, Darius, and another voice he didn't recognize. They all converged on the parlor and he felt Dr. Bishop's hands on his back near where he knew the knife was sticking.

"I need him moved to a table, and need towels and spirits, and every lamp you can muster,"

Bishop ordered brusquely. The servants scurried to do his bidding.

"NO! the vicar! I need the vicar first!" David cried out. Lying face down on the settee he could not see who was there. Suddenly the vicar came into his view, and knelt near his head.

"My son, what can I do for you?"

"Marry us, right now. I have the special license. I'll not let anyone touch me until we are wed." He insisted. He knew they all thought he was crazy but he didn't care. They weren't moving him, or operating on him until he made Clary his wife.

The vicar looked to Clary, who was wide eyed with anxiety. "Miss Clarissa, is this your desire? Do you wish to marry at this moment?"

"Yes, yes, of course. Quickly please!" She took his hand.

Without preamble the vicar went into an abbreviated ceremony, asking if they should take each other in sickness and in health, for richer or poorer, as long as they both shall live. They both agreed, and he declared them married. He felt the briefest kiss as Clarissa's lips touched his, then the doctor ordered her away and he felt another searing pain as he was lifted and placed on a hard surface in the center of the room. This time when the blackness came, with relief he gave in to it. Clarissa would be taken care of.

He could rest now.

Chapter Twenty-Five

Clarissa was pushed aside as they lifted David off the settee and placed him atop the long sideboard which had been moved to the center of the room. His agonized scream was cut short as he passed out, and she felt it like a wrench to her heart. How much pain must he be in to lose consciousness?

A dozen people filled the room, Darius and Lucas, the Doctor and a man that had come with him, as well as the vicar and several servants. All were following Dr. Bishops shouted orders, holding lamps and candles and towels, and bottles of spirits. Doctor Bishop had commandeered a side table and laid out several items from his black bag. Scalpels and what looked like a spreader of some sort, and several needles already threaded with stiff black thread. He took the bottle of spirits and poured it first over his own hands, then over the knife and wound.

Dr. Bishop looked in turn to Darius and Lucas and to his friend, and ordered them to hold David down and as still as possible, should he awaken. She prayed he would stay unaware until this ordeal was over as she knew the worst was yet to come.

Betty MacPherson was on the other side of the sideboard, with towels in her hands. He ordered her to be ready to staunch the wound the moment he pulled the knife out. The doctor counted "One, two, three!" and pulled the hilt of the knife from David's back. The blade was at least six inches long and had been plunged in to the hilt just under his shoulder blade at a downward angle. It came out dripping with blood and Clarissa felt faint with horror.

The sight of blood always did this to her, and to know it was David's blood…she took another step back until she hit the divan and sat down, shaking.

David had revived briefly, crying out, but Darius and Lucas held him down firmly. He seemed to lose consciousness again. Blood gushed from the wound and Betty quickly applied pressure to it with the towel, which reddened immediately. After a minute had passed the doctor had her lift up on the towel and he seemed to breathe a sigh of relief

"The bleeding is slowing, and no bubbles. So he has not had damage to the heart or lungs, I think somehow all the major organs have been missed, thank God." He leaned down and sniffed the oozing wound, and examined the towel that had just been applied "no stench of bowel at all, and no other matter coming up. That's very good. I just need to expand the cut and stitch it up from the inside out. I think the knife hit muscle and lodged in a rib, based on how hard I had to pull to get it out," he explained.

"Is that good?" Clarissa asked, standing again on shaking legs. Bishop continued to apply pressure to the wound and spared a glance at her to nod. Clarissa breathed a sigh of relief.

"He would have bled to death by now if it had gone into his heart or lungs. It may have hit his liver-but that organ is a bit more resilient, still I will need to open him up a bit more to sew him up. Miss Clarissa you may want to leave for this."

"I...no...if he..." her protests were cut short with a frustrated exclamation from the doctor.

"Darius please escort Miss Clarissa to the next room-I'm certain His Grace would not want her to see this," Dr. Bishop insisted.

Darius nodded, leaving his spot at David's head and went to Clarissa, firmly taking her by the arm and led her from the room, and down the corridor to the library. He pushed her into a chair and went to the tray of decanters on the side table and poured her a generous dram of brandy and handed it to her.

"Drink up." He insisted, and then poured himself a brandy as well, downing it in a single swallow. He sat down, next to Clarissa, and she noted that he his hands were shaking now, as badly as hers.

She took a long drought of the brandy and took several deep breaths, waiting for the warmth to overtake the coldness filling her, before asking the question that burned her. "Darius...what happened?"

"We were ambushed. We were nearly home, maybe less than a half hour from the estate. We were on the Drury Road, right after where it intersects to Branbury, under a copse of trees..."

"I know that area, the trees are so thick there, for at least a quarter mile, almost like a tunnel."

"Yes...the horses started to get anxious, rearing up. We all pulled our weapons. But the assailant was waiting for us in the trees. Leaped right down on top of him, we couldn't shoot, for fear of hitting his Grace. I tried to grab him, but the horses were all rearing and I just couldn't get close enough...and it was so dark...I saw the blade of the knife, then nothing. His Grace fought off the man, stabbing him a few times until he fell, and we all took off. I didn't realize until we were well away from the spot, that he had been stabbed as well...that the knife was still in him."

"So this man, the one who stabbed him, is dead?"

"I don't know...he fell to the ground. We did not want to stay in case there were others ready to continue where he left off, he may still be lying there, for all we know."

A knock to the doorway of the library brought both of their heads up; in the doorway was the man who had shown up with Dr. Bishop. He took a few steps into the library.

"Pardon me, Miss, Lt. Welch, I am Detective Percival Darwin, I'm with the London Metropolitan Police. I came to Dr. Bishop's request, arriving earlier today. I am sorry our meeting is not under better circumstances. May I ask you some questions? And also of you, Lt. Welch?" he asked, sitting down and taking a notebook from his coat pocket. Clarissa glanced towards Darius, and he nodded and she took a deep breath to brace herself.

"Of course, Detective Darwin."

"The initial attack with the highwaymen, did you recognize anything about those men? Had you possibly seen them before, in town or around the property?" he asked of Clarissa

"No, I'm certain of that. I'd never laid eyes on any of them before. I thought it was a random robbery, until one of the men was about to shoot David-His Grace, he had the gun to the Duke's head and he then said something about being glad he didn't have to share the reward now. That's when I...when I pulled the trigger, and shot him."

"You were very brave, Miss. It sounds like you

saved the life of His Grace. I understand that you had already sustained an injury to the head at that point."

"I did, although I didn't really know it. I thought I'd been hit by a rock or a pebble. I had no idea it was a bullet until I saw the blood. Sir, so you think that it was the same people behind the attack tonight?"

"I suspect so; it would be a strange coincidence for the incidents to be unrelated. Lt. Welch, what do you remember of the incident from tonight?" he asked. Darius related the same story that he had previously told Clarissa. Darwin frowned.

"This man, was he young, old, did he say anything?"

"No. just a bit of grunting as they were fighting. I think that second stab His Grace took to him, may have done him in. If he's not dead, he soon will be," Darius guessed. Darwin nodded.

"If you are able, I would like to go back to the scene, tonight. Lt. Welch, would you be willing to take me there? If the suspect is still alive, I am in hopes that he may be able to answer some questions. If not, hopefully there will be something on his person that may help answer our questions." Darius looked to Clarissa, uncertain whether he should leave her alone. She reached out and took his hand and gave it a reassuring squeeze.

"I'll be fine, Darius. Please, go with Detective

Darwin. I fear time is of the essence here, and he needs your assistance more than I."

"I'll come back as soon this is dealt with, Miss Clarissa...Your Grace, that is." She startled, she hadn't made the connection. She was married. She was now the Duchess. This brought to mind, the Duchess upstairs. She prayed she was sleeping through all of it, but thought it best to check. Knowing Drusilla, she'd try to make her way down the stairs and hurt herself if it meant getting to David.

Clarissa stood, and made her leave, running towards the stairs, the gentlemen also left, going out the front door.

Chapter Twenty-Six

Clarissa saw a light shining under the door of Drusilla's room, and without knocking, opened the door. The Duchess was sitting up in bed, her legs thrown over the edge as if preparing to stand. She breathed a sigh of frustrated relief at the sight of Clarissa. "What is going on, Clarissa? I have rang and rang for help and no one is coming, I could hear a commotion..."

Without any forethought, Clarissa ran to the Duchess and fell to her knees in front of her, and burst into tears. Drusilla wrapped her arms around her and Clarissa clung to her, needing desperately to feel her mother's arms about her now.

"Clarissa, what is it? What happened?"

"Oh...mother...mother...David's been stabbed." She gasped. She felt Drusilla stiffen and then wrap her, even closer in her frail arms.

"Is he...is he gone?" The Duchess whispered. Clarissa shook her head.

"No...Dr. Bishop is working on him. He was stabbed over three miles from here, and they rode here, him with the knife sticking from his back. He refused to let the doctor take care of him until the vicar married us...so...we married in a minute-long ceremony, while his wound bled. If he doesn't live...I can't bear it. How did you bear it, so many years ago?"

"I don't know that I did. I had you to think about, and then David, so I moved on, one day after the next. That is all a person can do. But, if he is alive now, there is hope. I have faith in Dr. Bishop, and faith that God would not dare to take another person I love from me, in my final days." The Duchess said.

"Mother...I am so terrified."

"You call me mother, and it is like my fondest dream come true, at the moment my worst nightmare comes before me. That Lord Grey will come to take it all away."

"If he is behind this, I swear I will kill him myself." Clarissa swore.

"He is desperate, and desperate men make mistakes. We will be vindicated. I have to believe that."

"I don't even care about it...none of it. The estate or the money, or the title, I never have. I've always felt glad that it was David, and not I that had to deal with it all. That was so selfish of me... if he'd been left to grow up as George and Annabelle's son...he'd be whole now and not fighting for his life..."

"It pains me to say that you are most assuredly right. He has been my son, since the day of his birth, just as you have been the daughter of my heart and body. I thought...I fear I used him, to save us from ruin, but have ruined him in the process. I thought handing him a fortune and a title could make up for any lie...I was so very wrong. Clarissa I don't know if he could ever forgive me, or if you should."

"There is nothing to forgive. It is the situation we are in, and the one we must live with. If... When David lives, if he wants to give up the duchy, I will stand beside him in his decision. I would rather have nothing and him by my side, than a castle and live in it alone."

"I have lived in that castle, alone, my dear, and it is a sad and lonely place. I would not wish that for you, either." Clarissa basked in the feel of Drusilla, stroking her hair until she felt calm and the tears finally ceased. Getting to her feet, reluctantly she let go of the Duchess's hands.

"I must go check on him...I will keep you apprised of his condition." She promised the Duchess. She nodded and wiped away the last of the tears from her own face.

"Yes...I should try to sleep a bit, I'm sure tomorrow will be a difficult day, no matter what it brings."

"I...am sorry you did not get to see us wed."

"It is probably best, I missed that, and I am not sure how I would have handled seeing him in that state. I demand a proper ceremony, at your first convenience, as soon as David is up to it."

"I can agree to that...I was so looking forward to wearing your dress, and seeing David's eyes when he saw me in it."

"He will have his chance. We must believe that." They bade each other goodnight and Clarissa went back downstairs. She was nearly terrified to peek into the sitting room off the foyer where the operation still went on. She stuck her head inside and was reassured that David was still alive and that the Doctor appeared to be in the process of sewing up his wound. Lucas still had his body half draped over David, holding him down, though it appeared he was clearly out cold. Several towels and rags covered in blood, had fallen to the floor, and the sight made her queasy. She stepped away from the room and sat down on a narrow bench in the hallway, and waited for the Doctor to finish his work. It was a good hour before the doctor stepped into the hallway, wiping his brow, and his hands on a towel. He sat down on the bench next to Clarissa and took her hand in his.

"I think, barring infection, we have saved him. These next forty-eight hours are critical. I will stay here. I have giving him laudanum to keep him from moving and tearing up his stitches. We must watch him for fever and keep an eye on the wound to make sure it does not turn on us. For now, I am...optimistically hopeful," Clarissa nodded and leaned against the doctor. He wrapped his arm around her. "I can't believe you married him," Bishop said on an incredulous tone. She shrugged.

"I love him...I always have," she said, simply.

"I never stood a chance, did I?" he surmised.

"I'm sorry..."

"I'm a man grown, I will live. And I suspect, so will your husband."

"My husband, I never thought to hear that word."

"You had best get used to it, Cissy. Or shall I call you Your Grace, now."

"Never...you are my dear, dear friend. You may address me any way you wish."

"I hope I always retain that position, as your dear, dear friends. You are mine, as well, my sweet Miss Clarissa," he said. "And because you are so dear to my heart, I would not dare to break yours. I vow to you to heal your husband."

"Thank you, Reggie."

"He will probably be out for several hours. I am having a bed brought down to the parlor, to avoid moving him as much as possible. You can go see him now. Mind he is very pale; he has lost much blood. Then I demand you get some sleep, you will need it."

"I will do that. I saw the duchess. You may want to peek in on her. I fear I cried over her like a watering pot when I saw her. She seemed to handle it well, but I worry..."

"I will look in on her. All my patients under one roof, how convenient for me," he said dryly, and she felt the corner of her mouth quirk in a near smile, which surprised her.

"I will request a room be made up for you, as well. You will need your rest too," she insisted.

Just as she was saying that they heard a ruckus at the front entry. Both Reginald and Clarissa jumped up and rushed down the hall, to find Darius, and Detective Darwin carrying a bloody body between them. Going to them she was shocked to her core to see, that the body they carried was Robbie MacPherson, the son of MacPherson and Betty.

"Oh my God, what happened?" she cried.

"We went back to the scene of the crime and found him, crawled off in the bushes," Darius explained. "He's still alive, but just barely. Can you give us a hand here, Doc?"

"Of course...in here," he said, directing them into the parlor across the hall from the one that now held David. As they laid Robbie out on the settee the doctor ran across the hall for his bag and came back quickly. Percival had already begun the work of stripping the boy down, when

Betty came into the room.

"Oh my gracious, my boy! What has happened? Was he attacked too?"

"Madam...we suspect he is the one that attacked His Grace," the detective stated regretfully

"What? No...no, that cannot be, Robbie would never do such a thing. This isn't true!" his mother insisted and turned towards Clarissa, beseechingly, who could only look back with an equal look of bewildered shock. Bishop called for assistance.

Lucas came from the other room, and quickly assessed the situation. With firm authority he led Betty out of the room and called for another maid to come and assist the doctor.

Clarissa sat down on a chair in the room in shock. Robbie, had attacked David? He'd grown up in the house; he'd been like family to her, like a little brother to her and David. Why would he do such a thing? She couldn't even fathom this reality. Was it possible he was just a victim, like David had been? Or horrible as that seemed, she hoped that was the truth. The idea that Robbie MacPherson had attempted to kill David was a horror to gruesome to comprehend.

Bishop worked frantically, staunching the flow of blood. He pulled off his own belt and wrapped it around Robbie's upper arm, then looked around frantically before plucking a silver candlestick off a table and wrapping it under the belt he twisted it several times, creating a tourniquet. He gestured to Clarissa, who shook off her frozen countenance and went to the doctor's side.

"Hold this," he directed, and then quickly grabbed the rip in the sleeve and ripped the material open the length of the arm. She had to look away at the deep gash on Robbie's arm that appeared to go down to the bone. Bishop poured spirits into the wound and Robbie's body seized and his eyes popped open, looking directly at Clarissa.

"I'm sorry...I'm sorry..." he gasped before his eyes rolled back in his head and he slumped down again. Bishop went to work stitching the gash shut and directed a maid to apply pressure to the wound in the boys left torso. As soon as he was done stitching he released the tourniquet and then went to work on work on the wound in the boy's side.

Clarissa held a lantern aloft to give him light but tried not to look at what he was doing any more than she had to. She started to shake and when Lucas came back and took the lantern away from her, she let him have it without complaint. She stepped back and back again, until she found herself in the other parlor across the hall. She turned to see David, in a makeshift bed, lying still with nothing but a sheet covering his lower half.

He lay on his stomach, the red bandaged wound stark against the pale skin of his back. She went to him and pulled a chair next to his bed and clasped his hand. His eyes opened blearily and she tried to smile.

"Clary..." he murmured. "Love...you."

"I know I love you too, David, so much. Save your strength, and go back to sleep." She whispered. His eyes closed again and she knew he was back to the world of oblivion. She heard a commotion from the parlor across the hall as MacPherson entered, in an obvious state of upset. She spared a glance as she saw Percival Darwin drag MacPherson out of the room bodily and down the hall, she guessed to the library.

At the moment, she could barely spare a moment to care what that was about. All her thoughts were about the man on the cot in front of her, and she prayed, with everything she had in her, that he would live.

Chapter Twenty-Seven

Percival Darwin dragged the struggling MacPherson into the library and shut the door. "My good man, I must ask you to calm yourself," he advised. MacPherson wrenched away from him and went for the door but Darwin blocked him easily.

"My boy is hurt! I need to be with my son."

"Sir, in this state you'd only interfere with the doctor's efforts. You will see your son, but I must ask if you know of any reason why Robbie would want to harm His Grace?

"What...what do you mean?"

"We have reason to believe that he was the one who attacked the Duke of Hollister tonight."

"No...no! That can't be. He doesn't even know...has nothing to do with...no..." MacPherson denied.

Darwin had been watching MacPherson's face closely, as a myriad of emotions crossed it, he saw that MacPherson didn't want to believe his son could do such a thing, but he also saw that the man knew more than he was saying."

"What or who doesn't your son know, Mr. MacPherson?" he asked.

MacPherson took a step back and clenched his fists, like he was dying to bash something or someone. Then it was as if, in an instant, all the fight left him, leaving him deflated.

"Lord Grey...I don't know how, but I think Lord Grey must have coerced Robbie into doing this. There could be no other explanation."

"What makes you think this?" Darwin asked.

MacPherson paced the room, summoning up the courage to tell the truth, hoping against hope he was not making a mistake, going against Lord Grey, but he had had enough.

"The man has been a thorn in my side since I was a boy myself, much younger than Robbie." He confessed "He's been blackmailing me for more than 25 years. I've been...giving him information about the goings on, here at Hollister."

"Did you know he intended to attack the Duke of Hollister, the first time, when he and Miss Clarissa were coming back from London? Or this time?"

"No...I swear. I told him...I told him that Miss Clarissa and I were going to go fetch His Grace from London, but that was all. Over the years, I've told him so many things, and nothing ever comes of it. I had no reason to think that time he'd plan anything around it. I swear I never said a word, this time about his going to London again. I would never have involved my son. Never! You have to believe that!"

"I can only take your word for it. You believe that Lord Grey may have approached your son?"

"I...I don't know how...I've been careful, never said a word to my wife or Robbie about him. I can only think Robbie must have followed me. That last time, I saw Grey was at a tavern in the next village over in the next county. I tried to break free of him, refused to give him any more information. But he threatened me, and my wife and son if I didn't. I started making up falsehoods to tell him about the Duchess getting well and David deciding to go back to London to live after all. I think...he must have known I was lying and decided that Robbie would be more apt to do his bidding."

"I've been told that this Lord Grey was suspected of being behind the killings of the Duke's father, and his footman, twenty-five years ago. Do you know anything about that?" Percival leveled a hard eyed stare at MacPherson, who seemed to crumble before his eyes. The man sat down heavily in a chair and took his hat off, ringing it in his hands.

"Yes. He was behind it. I was just a boy; I didn't know..."

"Start at the beginning. How did you meet Lord Grey?"

"My father died when I was a wee babe and my mother, she worked herself to an early grave. By the time I was ten, she was gone and I was on the street. You have to know, hunger and cold can drive even the most honorable person to do things, and I was so young. I got in with a gang of boys, like myself, and we would break into the empty houses and…steal. I was small for my age then, and able to get in through the chimney, as long as it wasn't lit. I would get in, then go open the door for the other boys and we'd go about and take whatever we could sell, or eat and be off. One night, I came into a house and when I come out of the chimney, Lord Grey was waiting there for me, and grabbed me."

"Caught you in the act, and used it to his advantage, I take it?"

"I thought…I thought he actually wanted to help me, he said he could get a job for me, a paying job in a nice house and all I would have to do is keep an eye on things, tell him what the goings on were, there. It didn't seem like such a bad thing, at least that's what I thought at the time. He said if I didn't do it, he'd take me to the constable himself and turn me in for trespassing and theft. He told me I'd hang, as he was an Earl, and a friend of Prinny himself. It seemed like an easy enough thing to do. He got me hired on as a tiger at his nephew's home, the Duke of Hollister-Dorian Thoroughgood. I loved working for the Duke, he was kindness, itself. I worked in the stables, and helped with the horses and learned so much. George, the head footman was particularly kind to me. He had served with the old Duke during the war, and the Duke had hired him after-they were good friends.

"We met every few weeks, back then. He said he just wanted to make sure that the Duke was not having any trouble. I believed him. I would tell him of the things I knew. Reported whatever gossip I heard. I never really thought anything of it. The Duke had wanted to buy a new team of horses and had scheduled a trip to Tattersalls auction, for him and the Duchess. I was most excited as the Duke had promised me my own horse, and even said I could pick it out. I reported this to Lord Grey. I had no idea...I didn't know what he had planned. You have to believe me," MacPherson swore.

"I understand you were quite young at that time, and I believe that you had no foreknowledge of the events that would occur."

"That's right. Truly, I would never have told him, never have breathed about that trip if I knew..."

"Go on, Mr. MacPherson, what happened after that."

"Well, the Duchess ended up not going; I believe she was feeling poorly. She was with child at the time, you know. The Duke went, and George and I, just the three of us. The men, there were several of them, came out of nowhere, all of them had guns. George was ordered to stop. He yelled at me to run and he jumped down and was fighting them. The Duke was pulled from the carriage. A man had his gun pointed right at the Duke and George, he...he jumped in front of him. He was shot, and shot again, and then the Duke was shot. Then, I saw Lord Grey come out from behind some trees and he called to me, and he...he threatened me. He said if I told anyone he was involved he would make sure that I would hang for being a thief, as well as conspiring to kill the Duke. I believed him. He told me what to say, and I did. I went to the Duchess and Miss Annabelle- she was George's wife and told them exactly what he told me to say. I thought that would be the end of it but no, it was just a beginning. Every month for years I've had to report the goings on here. Not that there has been much to tell. Most months there really was nothing to report at all. And nothing really came of it, not in the longest time. I should never have forgotten. I shouldn't have told him about Miss Clarissa going to London to bring the Duke back. I...it's my fault what happened to them. I think that Lord Grey would have had me killed too, if it weren't for the Duke and Miss Clarissa taking matters into their own hands and killing those men. Lord Grey came to me afterwards...I decided right then I was done cooperating with him, I wasn't going to feed him any more information. I had no idea...I should have known he would go after my son. Robbie, he's a good boy, I swear it. I can only imagine what Lord Grey would have threatened him with to get him to do this. He isn't to blame. If anyone needs to hang for this, it's me," MacPherson insisted.

Darwin gave him a considering look. It was quite a story the man had told him but he could clearly see the guilt and remorse, and more importantly the relief that unburdening the truth brought to the man. He had hidden knowledge of a crime that had gone unsolved for decades, not to mention the crimes against the current Duke and his new wife. He was also one of the few who knew what Lord Grey looked like now.

"I do not know what will happen with your son, I have documented what you have told me, and with your sworn statement, we may be able to put an end to this. We will need your help. Are you willing to help us?"

"Anything, I will do anything; just...please let my son go."

"That will be for the court to decide, but anything you do to help us will be to your and your son's advantage."

"Tell me what I need to do."

Chapter Twenty-Eight

The morning had been an exercise in frustration. People came and went, but no one would tell him anything. He had a vague recollection of hearing something the night before, while he was drifting in and out of consciousness after Bishop had operated on him. Some sort of altercation, Bishop rushing into the room and grabbing his bag and raised voices. Something happened, but everyone was being very closemouthed about it. When he asked Bishop about it, when he'd come to check him at dawn, he was told to concentrate on his own recovery and just know that everything else was being handled. At the time he was still dazed to argue, but now he felt more alert, and did not take kindly to being kept in the dark any longer.

Clarissa came into the room, bearing a tray with some broth and tea. He carefully turned from his stomach to his side and winced as the movement pulled at his stitches. He wondered how long it would be before he could accomplish any movement without pain.

"I brought you some broth. Reggie said if you keep this down you can have some solid food later. How are you feeling?" she said, setting the tray down on the table in front of the settee. He struggled to sit up, and she went to him to help him. He felt a bit lightheaded and weak. The wound in his back was a source of constant, dull pain, unless he moved then it was a jabbing presence.

"Fine," he assured her. "I feel fine." She rolled her eyes, at his words.

"Liar."

"Well, I am alive and I don't know that I have the luxury of complaining, considering there was a time last night when I felt I might not be here to see the morning. I am quite happy to be proven wrong."

"I did make it a condition for marrying you that you would live. I am glad to see that you lived up to your end of the bargain."

"I apologize that it was not the wedding night that I had wanted to give you. I will make it up to you as soon as I am able," He promised. She leaned over and kissed him lingeringly, then drew back with a smile.

"I shall hold you to that, Your Grace."

"I am going to institute a rule, nay, and a law in our marriage. When we are alone, I am never,

ever, to be addressed as Your Grace."

"Shall I call you Sir, or Lord Master of all that he surveys?" she teased.

"The only title I truly want is that of beloved husband." He took her hand in his and drew her down next to him on the settee. He wished he could pull her closer still, but she was sitting on the side of his injury and lifting that arm was more than he could bear at the moment. Still, with his opposite hand He lifted her palm to his lips and kissed it. She sighed and leaned a bit against him. He didn't dare complain that the movement caused him pain.

"You will always be my beloved husband. And I hope I shall always be your adoring and beloved wife. I will happily abide by this law." She smiled. She reached for the broth and he reluctantly let go of her hand. She intended to spoon it into his mouth, and he balked..

"I can feed myself," he insisted. She set the bowl down again and gave him a look.

"Prove it." He reached for the spoon; A jabbing pain to his shoulder had him remembering the injury was to his right shoulder blade, his dominant arm. He changed tactics and used his left hand, and realized he did not have the coordination, nor the strength, to raise it to his lips, and sloshed it down his front before it made it to his mouth.

"Fine, I could use a bit of help," he admitted reluctantly. She gave him a knowing, superior smirk, one he'd seen many times growing up, whenever she would best him at anything. It should have made him angry, but oddly, it filled him with joy. His Clary, the girl he had always loved was right here beside him, and pain aside, he could not be happier.

She guided the spoon to his mouth and he obediently opened for her. He eyed her intently, as she fed him, spoonful after spoonful of the broth.

Somehow, the act had taken on an erotic intimacy. She would bite her lower lip as she lifted each spoonful, then as it reached his mouth, she would open her own lips, almost unconsciously mimicking him, licking them as she removed the spoon.

She did this time and again, and he felt himself grow hard, as he could only imagine other ways she could use that mouth on him. When the bowl was empty she set it aside.

The atmosphere in the room was charged. He was in a quandary, wanting his wife, and not being in a position to do anything about it. She glanced down to his lap, where a bulge was prominently displayed. A rosy blush came to her cheeks and a sly look entered her eyes. She got up, and for a moment he thought she was leaving, as she was heading towards the door of the parlor. Instead she shut the doors, and flicked the lock.

She came back to him, and gracefully knelt on the floor, between his legs.

"Let me take care of you." With shaking fingers, she unbuttoned the fall of his breeches, extracted his cock, and began stroking it. His head fell back in ecstasy at her touch. She directed him to lie down on his left side again and she continued her ministration, stroking him gently at first, then with more force.

He remembered when they were sixteen and he had taught her how to touch him like this. Did he dare ask for more? He desperately wanted to feel her mouth on him, but could not ask it of her. As if sensing this, she hesitantly leaned forward and gave a kiss to the tip. He groaned and she took that as encouragement, and took the head into her mouth, licking and sucking, taking him deeper.

He was leaning on his left arm, and unable to use his right, but he ached to twine his fingers through her hair and guide her deeper. She seemed to understand and began bobbing her head, taking him deeper with each advance, until he touched the back of her throat. She pumped him with one hand and caressed his tightening balls with the other. He was so close...so close.

"Love...I'm going to spend." He warned, at the last moment, expecting her to pull away. But she surprised him by taking him deeper still, and his essence spurted down her throat as she swallowed him down.

Withdrawing, she lovingly licked his softening cock, cleaning it of all traces of his desire, and then with little ceremony, she pulled up his fall and buttoned him back up. He lay slumped on his side, feeling completely sated, and abnormally weak and a bit dizzy, but he didn't dare complain. He wished he was in a state where he could return the favor but he was done in.

Later, when he got his strength back, he would make sure she was pleasured and satisfied beyond her wildest dreams. That thought alone would hasten his recovery, he was certain.

"You did not need to do that," he assured her, "but I am most gratified that you did."

"I wanted to. Remember when we were children and we found that book in the stable, with the illustrations?"

"Awww, yes...MacPherson's secret treasure trove, hid under the haystack. I remember we couldn't have been more than nine or ten at the time."

"And we looked at each page of drawings of men and women doing all sorts of naughty things to each other, and giggled, and said we would never do such things! Can I confess now; I want to do all of those things with you?"

"I recall that what you just did was illustrated on page five of that masterpiece."

"I am especially looking forward to acting out

pages ten through fifteen." She told him, picking up the tray, with a flirtatious tone. He tried to recall, then remembered it was a variety of female dominant positions, that had confused him and excited him mightily at the time. He did not tell her that after finding that hidden book, he had returned to the stable quite often, alone, to peruse those pages. He grinned at her, and enjoyed the blush to her skin, as she confessed her desire to try these things.

"I promise you, I will be your willing subject to act out every one of those pages, as soon as I am able. I look quite forward to it."

"As do I," she smiled.

Now that they were both presentable, she went to the doorway and unlocked the door, surprised to find Percival Darwin and Reginald Bishop on the other side. She turned shocked eyes towards David, and he could see that she was wondering how much they had overheard. Her pink cheeks went scarlet but she recovered nicely. He tried to sit up again, but found he was incapable of that simple action, so remained, lying on his side.

"I regret that I was not able to introduce you last night, Your Grace. This is my friend, Percival Darwin. He is the detective the London Metropolitan Police."

"Good Morning, Detective Darwin, I apologize that I am unable to get up at the moment."

"Certainly, no apology is necessary, Your Grace. We do have news that may be of interest to you. We have evidence that Lord Grey was indeed behind both attacks on you, and was in fact behind the attack on your father, twenty-five years ago."

"Was he the one that stabbed me last night?"

"No...but it was someone in your household, you know."

"What? How can that be? Who would do such a thing?"

"The assailant, last night, was one Robert MacPherson."

"Robbie? But, he's just a boy! Why would he do something like this?"

"He was coerced, as we understand it, Lord Grey has evidence of a crime that his father committed a number of years ago, and threatened the life of his father, as well as his mother. He was acting under the instruction, of Lord Grey, to attack you."

"I stabbed him back, is he alive?"

"He is. Percival and Darius went back to the sight of the attack last night and found him and brought him back. I was able to stitch up his wounds, but I daresay he is in worse shape than you. He is under arrest but unable to be moved right now. He is locked in the salon across the hall."

"I don't understand how did he know that

Lord Grey was behind the crime from twenty-five years ago?"

"MacPherson confessed that he has been feeding information to Lord Grey since he has been in the employ of this family. Lord Grey has been blackmailing him. MacPherson had been caught him stealing when he was a child, and has been holding that over him all these years, and that is why he had been feeding information back to him. I think that this incident with his son has changed his feelings on the matter, and he has offered himself up to help trap Lord Grey, if you are willing to drop the charges against his son."

"His son nearly killed me!"

"True, but he has no real malice towards you. As I understand it, Lord Grey was threatening both his father and mothers' lives, if he did not cooperate with his scheme. MacPherson has offered full cooperation in return for letting his boy go free. He has offered to send him away to America, and you would never have to see him again."

"I suppose I can agree to that. I don't know what to think about this. MacPherson has been with this house since before I was born. He used to tell me stories about my father. He taught me to ride a horse, how to hammer a nail. I can't bear the thought that he was betraying me, betraying my mother and Clarissa the whole time."

"He is willing to talk to you, he and Robbie

both. I can arrange that, if you'd like." Darwin told him. David looked towards Clarissa, where she sat perched on the edge of a chair across from him. She looked as stricken as he felt. She'd always had a great fondness for MacPherson, and Robbie. He remembered how she use to take Robbie about the garden by the hand when he was a toddler and show him all the flowers, and how she loved to play with him, like he was the little brother she never had. This has to be especially difficult for her.

"What do you think?" he asked her.

"I don't know. It is a terrible thing, what they have both done, but we know them, we grew up with them, like an extended part of our family. I don't think MacPherson or Robbie is evil, or malicious. I think, they were being manipulated and used and forced to do things that were against their natures to protect each other and to protect Betty. Should either of them hang for that?" She asked. David tried to think of the Robbie he has known as a baby and small boy, and the Robbie he knew now as a sixteen-year-old teenager. He remembered being that age, when he too, also acted without thinking of the consequences. He did not want Robbie or MacPherson to hang.

"I will talk to them, and if they are willing to help trap Lord Grey, I will drop the charges," he decided.

"Very well, I will arrange for you all to talk."

"I think that His Grace has had quite enough to deal with at the moment. I demand he have at least a few hours' rest before he goes through that ordeal," Bishop stated.

"I agree; David needs to rest. Besides, I think the Duchess has a right to be part of this as well. I would like to have her brought down." Clarissa stated.

"I don't know that Mother needs to hear all this in her condition," David protested.

"I think, no, I know that she has been haunted for years about her husband's death. I think knowing all the facts at last will give her some peace, and I think that knowing that something is being done to avenge him at last, will ease her mind. I am certain in her place; I would feel the same way."

"Very well, when she is able, we will all confront them together."

Chapter Twenty-Nine

It was three hours later when they were all brought together in the parlor that Robbie MacPherson was recovering in. As Clarissa had expected, the Duchess had demanded she be present for this event. David had even felt able to walk the few steps across the hallway, and now sat in a chair. The Duchess reached out and took her sons hand, as if assuring herself that he was indeed alive. Percival Darwin and Reginald Bishop were also present.

MacPherson was there as well, and Betty insisted that she be present to give both her son and husband support. Once they were all gathered an awful silence filled the room. MacPherson sat forward in his chair, wringing his ever present wool cap in his hand. He cleared his throat then, and stood up, and looked at both the Duchess and David, and Clarissa.

"I...I have been keeping a secret from you, since the day I started working for the old duke when I was a boy," he confessed. "I did a bad thing, and I was caught by Lord Grey, and he threatened me, told me I'd hang unless I co-operated. Robbie here, had nothing to do with it, it was all me." He insisted.

"Papa, don't do this," Robbie gasped, one arm was in a sling, the other grasping his side in pain.

"I've been told you know something about the day David and Clarissa's fathers were murdered," The Duchess stated.

MacPherson nodded, tears gathering in his eyes, and a look of misery and shame like none that Clarissa had ever witnessed before. Whatever he did or knew she was certain there was no malicious or evil intent dwelling within this man.

"It's true, Your Grace. If you remember, you were supposed to make the trip with us that day," he said, directing his words to Drusilla.

"That's right, but I was feeling poorly, I was halfway through my confinement at that time."

"For months, I had been reporting the comings and goings to Lord Grey. We would meet down at the end of the Post Road at noon every Thursday. I would meet him there and tell him the latest gossip from the servants or whatever the latest news was. I…I told him about the trip to Tattersalls. I swear to you, I had no idea what he had planned. I'd given him information for months and never knew why he wanted it. I never thought to ask. If I had known…I swear I would have never said a word. You have to believe that," MacPherson declared. Tears now freely fell from the man's eyes.

Clarissa wasn't sure how to feel. This man, someone she had great affection for, was one of the reasons she had grown up without a father. If the Duke Dorian had lived, she and David would never have been switched. She would have grown up with the privileges of being a Dukes daughter, might have had brothers and sisters.

Might not have had David...if things had been different, she would never have been allowed to marry the son of the footman and the ladies' maid.

She couldn't regret that.

"Was anything you told me that day, true?" The Duchess whispered.

"It was all true, the way it happened. George was...shot first, trying to protect the Duke, and then they killed him. I really didn't get the best look at the men's faces. I had run off into the woods at the edge of the road, as George had told me to do, but I saw...I saw...everything. It wasn't until I saw Lord Grey come out from behind a big tree that I realized he had been behind it all. He ordered I come out then...then he threatened me. He told me if I breathed a word I'd be hanged and I believed him. I realize, I still should have told you. I have no excuse for keeping silent all these years, just...I was so young, and then I met Betty and Robbie came along. I couldn't risk leaving them alone."

"You kept giving him information, even after what he did to my father," David asked, to clarify. MacPherson nodded, his eyes filled with guilt.

"I...I did. The day you two were born...he had demanded that I let him know as soon as the Duchess had her babe. I did, but I didn't tell him what the infant was, I pretended I didn't know. That's why he came."

"The man nearly killed David in his crib," The Duchess declared

"I'm ever so sorry, Your Grace."

"I am angry; MacPherson, but I, more than anyone knows how Lord Grey can drive a person mad. He tried to manipulate Dorian before, and during our marriage. I can only assume that when Dorian refused to give him what he wanted, which was control of the money, he decided we were disposable," The Duchess bitterly surmised as she shook her head in dismay.

"He and Dorian grew up together; they were like brothers, although I think the feeling was rather one-sided. I believe that Lord Grey resented Dorian, always. Dorian was more personable and well liked, and next in line after his older brother. Dorian went off to war, and while he was gone, his brother died under mysterious circumstances. I firmly believe that Lord Grey had something to do with that, although I've never had any actual proof. I suppose Lord Grey hoped

Napoleon would take care of Dorian for him. But he did not. Lord Grey was supposed to safeguard the estate until Dorian's return, instead he drove it to near ruin," the duchess said, and then took a long sip of her tea before she continued.

"I met Lord Grey at a ball, and he took a liking to me. I think he thought I was one who could be easily manipulated. He knew I had a dowry that could bring the estate back into the black. He convinced me to come to a house party, here at Hollister House, and meet the Duke. I had no real wish to marry, but my father was in failing health and seemed intent on having me marry before his demise. So I went, and I met my beloved Dorian. Within months we were engaged. At our betrothal ball, Lord Grey cornered me; he seemed to think my getting engaged to Dorian was my way of getting closer to himself, that I had fallen in with some grand plan he had to enrich himself. I quickly disabuse him of that notion. He grew angry and struck me. I ran away from him. I never told Dorian, but I knew...I knew that Lord Grey saw my actions, as a betrayal, and somehow he would make me pay. The death of my husband, and the husband of my dearest friend, was apparently not enough for him."

"Robbie, explain to us what happened this week. How did you come to be waiting for the Duke on the road," Percival asked the boy, who lay inclined on the settee. Robbie, looked first towards his mother, then towards his father, who gave him a solemn nod."

"Last week, I saw Papa leave in the middle of the day. He'd just come home a few days before hand and had been roughed up a bit, you know. I was worried about him. He'd been acting strangely too, since he'd been back. So, I followed him. He went into the tavern and I snuck in and sat so that I was behind him and had my back to him but I was close enough I could hear a bit. The man with the beard came in and sat down. I heard Papa tell him he wasn't going to give him any more information, then the man threatened to hurt my mother, and me if he didn't keep cooperating. He said he'd make sure Papa hanged. I...I couldn't let that happen. The man left and I followed him. I thought I would just see where he was going, but then he turned around and confronted me," the boy said, his voice quavering.

"Oh, Robbie," Betty murmured, horrified. He spared a glance up at her, and took a deep breath.

"I told him...I told him to leave my family alone and to leave the Duke alone and he just laughed. Then he grabbed me by the front of my shirt and threw me down to the ground and put a knife to my throat." MacPherson and Betty both gasped and David looked about the room, no one could doubt that Robbie was speaking the truth.

"Go on," David encouraged.

"He said he knew my father was lying, that

he knew that the Duchess was not getting better like he said that Papa was no longer useful to him and that he had to get rid of him. I knew he meant that he was going to kill him. He had the coldest eyes I was certain he meant it."

"Robbie boy, why didn't you come to me?" MacPherson cried out in anguish.

"Papa, what would you have done? The man threatened Ma'am and me. If you killed him you'd hang for sure. I couldn't let that happen."

"So you offered to kill me instead?" David asked. Robbie shook his head.

"That wasn't what happened. I pleaded with him, to leave Papa and Ma'am alone. He said if I did as he said, he'd never bother Papa again. He just wanted to know the next time you'd be away from Hollister House. When you came to me a few mornings ago and asked me to watch over the Welches place while you all went to London, I did tell him that you'd left town, and about when you were expecting to come back. He came up with the plan. I was supposed to be a look out, and give a whistle when you were approaching that stretch of the woods. There were two other men further up who had guns. I waited up in that tree for hours, and the longer I waited, the more I realized I couldn't do it. Finally, I saw you coming in the distance, and I tried to get out of the tree, and warn you, but my shirt got caught and I tried to pull free and was stuck, I got my knife out to saw my shirt away from the branch, finally it gave way and I ended up falling out of the tree on top of the Duke, and I still had the knife in my hand. I didn't mean to stab him. I swear I didn't! And I was just trying to grab him to hold on to keep from falling to the ground. Then I felt him jab me in the arm and in my side, then the next thing I knew I was on the dirt and they took off. I think all the commotion scared the shooters away. They never came back for me, I know that. I rolled off the road. I tried to get to my horse but... I couldn't mount him with my arm and my side like this. Then Mr. Welch and Mr. Darwin came and brought me here." Every eye was turned on Robbie in wide eyed amazement. Finally, Percival looked to Dr. Bishop.

"Reggie, in your medical opinion, is the wound consistent with a downward thrust that say, someone might cause by falling out of a tree."

"Well...thinking about it yes. It was at an angle and it definitely had a downward thrust from above as the knife blade was six inches long but only penetrated three inches deep, but for the entire length of the blade. It did cut into muscle and the tip lodged into the backside of a rib. If it had been plunged straight through from back to front it would have gone into his lung or possible his heart, luckily, it did not," Dr. Bishop surmised.

"So this stabbing saved me from a shooting?" David surmised. He wasn't sure how to feel about this. The moments of the stabbing had been so confusing, but with the explanation that Robbie gave, it could be true. He remembered grappling with the man, and looking back it did seem as if he had been trying to hang on more than anything. He had stabbed him the one time when he fell; it was David who had charged at him with his knife more than once.

"Do you believe this is what happened?" The Detective asked David. He reasoned out everything that he could remember. And then he looked at Robbie's face. He had known the boy since he was born, had spent considerable time with him since he had come home. There was nothing in the boy's face now that conveyed anything but the truth. Finally, he nodded.

"I believe him." He said. MacPherson and Betty as well as Clarissa all let out audible signs of relief. David looked towards Detective Darwin "So now we have irrefutable proof that Lord Grey has been behind the death of my father, as well as Clarissa's. Not to mention the two attempts on my life, and Clarissa and MacPherson's injuries. Surely this is enough to arrest the man and put him away?"

"It would be under normal circumstances. We are still dealing with the fact that it is the word of a commoner, or make those two commoners, against a peer. I hate to say that cases like this don't always go the way that we would like. If he could catch him in the act we'd be certain to be seeing him hang or be transported at the very least."

"How do we do that?" Clarissa asked the detective.

"We set a trap."

Chapter Thirty

The Tavern was nearly empty, Grey scanned the room, before selecting a table at the back corner, sending a nod to one of his cohorts, a few tables over as he sat down,

MacPherson had sent him a note to meet him here at 9:00 PM. It was a few minutes after, and the man wasn't here. Irritation ate at him.

Mac had better be telling him that the Duke was dead-or near enough. He'd been spying on the house for a few days and had seen a number of people come and go, but no sign of David-or of Mac's son Robbie.

Robbie was supposed to report to him after he attacked the Duke three nights ago, but had never shown up, so he had no idea what had happened. Was the boy arrested, had he run away? He'd wandered into the town and kept his ears open, thinking surely there would be some gossip about what had happened to the Duke, but he heard nothing. If anything at all had happened- and he was certain that something had, they were being quite secretive about it.

The tavern door squeaked open to reveal MacPherson. Spotting him, Mac waved and stopped at the counter to order ale, then casually made his way over. He appeared calm, although underneath Grey could sense that he was nervous, edgy.

Something was afoot, and it made Grey uneasy.

"Evenin' Guv'nor." MacPherson greeted as he plunked himself down opposite Grey.

"Mac, your note said you had news."

"Yes…the Duke and his mother are planning on going to Bath, the day after tomorrow. They'll be leaving at dawn, taking the northern route."

"So, the Duke is still alive?"

"Oh yes. Right as rain, he is. Had a bit of an altercation the other night on his way home from London, but nothing comes of it."

"He just decided to take his mother to Bath? What for?"

"Well, you know she'd been sickly. He heard that the baths were healing. He thought he'd give it a try, might stay a week, maybe more if she's feeling up to it."

"You're being rather forthcoming with information," Lord Grey said suspiciously.

"What you said last week about my family…I don't want them hurt. I figure the sooner this is all over with, the sooner they are safe," MacPherson shrugged.

"I see you've come to your senses, then."

"Yes Sir. My family means everything to me, as long as they are safe, I'll co-operate."

"I'm glad to hear it. And your son, Robbie is it? how is he?"

"Robbie? Well, funny you should mention him. He took off; we think he ran off with a girl from a neighboring town. He left a note that said he'd be back, so I'm sure he's fine."

"No warning? He simply left?"

"Robbie's always had a yearning to see the world. He is a grown man now, much as I hate to admit it. He can do as he pleases."

"I see," Grey nodded thoughtfully.

"It is most convenient; they will both be traveling together. What of the girl? The one he is so enamored with?"

"Oh. Miss Clarissa? She's not going. She and the Duke, well, it seems they agreed to part company. That's another reason for this trip, I think. He isn't much of a mind to be around her, now. You know the Duchess never did approve, and he doesn't want to go against his mother." MacPherson spoke quickly, and his voice had taken on an almost high pitched quality, and his eyes seemed to be shifting around as he talked. Mac was lying on the fly. Grey was sure of it. He pushed him again.

"I saw them rolling around together, rutting like dogs in heat, earlier this week. They seemed quite enamored with each other, then." Grey commented. Mac's eyes grew big and it was all Grey could do to not laugh at the man's befuddlement.

"I...I don't know about that. I never seen no such thing. Miss Clarissa's always been a real lady, leastways when I was around," Mac insisted.

"The Duke wouldn't be the first aristocrat to be sampling the house goods, I'm sure. A smart girl would find a way to take advantage of that."

"Now, I know'd Miss Clarissa since she was a wee babe. You can't be saying such things. She's a good girl, she is."

"I see you have a soft spot for the lady, pardon me, I didn't mean to get your dander up." Grey feigned in apology. Mac narrowed his eyes, sensing that Grey was putting him on, but let it go.

"I thank you for the information Mac..." Grey said, throwing a coin on the table towards MacPherson. "I'm sure that it will be quite useful."

MacPherson picked up the coin and placed it in his breeches pocket, and stood, bowing his head as he departed.

Grey sat and nursed his ale for a bit, and another man came to the table, one who had been sitting but a few feet away, while he conversed with MacPherson.

"That the bloke we'll be following? Day after tomorrow, he said?"

"No…no, we have a change of plans. We aren't going to do that. I sense it is a trap. We strike tomorrow."

"Strike? Strike where?"

"The house, robbed in broad daylight, tragic thing."

"You want I should round up a few more men?" The thug asked.

"Please do, all armed to the teeth, if you will. I am not letting the Duke or his bitch of a mother escape this time."

"Aye Sir." the man said. Lord Grey reached into his pocket and pulled out his roll of ten pound notes. He pulled off two hundred pounds, and handed it over, "Another two hundred when the job done, and a hundred-pound bonus to the man who kills the Duke, got that?"

"Aye, we'll get the job done Sir." The man said, giving him a lascivious grin, with a few teeth missing. Grey resisted the urge to shudder. Once he was Duke, he'd have no need to be associating with these lowlifes again. That day couldn't come soon enough.

Chapter Thirty-One

David gritted his teeth as he clutched the banister in a death grip. Now that he had made it all the way down the stairs, he was rethinking his idea to ignore the doctors' orders. He should have stayed in bed. It was four days since the assault, and the stab wound in his back still throbbed. The pull of the stitches, both internal and external were a whole other kind of pain.

Reginald had been by the previous evening and assured him that there was no sign of infection. The wound was healing, but advised him to avoid doing anything strenuous; citing a further tear in any of the inner injuries could lead to him bleeding to death. Of course, he had said this in front of Clarissa, who took his words to heart. After carefully climbing the stairs last night, hoping to finally enjoy a night in his wife's arms, she had held him off in fear of worsening his injury.

He had to wonder if Reggie was indulging in a bit of payback for marrying Clarissa out from under him, assuring he wouldn't be able to indulge in any amorous activities for the foreseeable future. He had spent a restless and frustrating night, in his Clarissa's arms, unable to consummate his marriage, as he wished.

"Are you certain you feel up to being about?" Clarissa asked, hovering on the stairs, next to him. " Maybe another few days abed are in order."

"I told you, I'm feeling better. I can't stand another day trapped indoors. I need to get out, get some fresh air at least. I promise if I feel fatigued, I'll take myself right back to bed."

"Alright, are you sure you don't need help? You can lean on me, you know." She said. He'd already shaken off her assisting arm at the top of the stairs, and now two steps from the bottom, he was determined to make it under his own steam. He shook his head and she stepped around him, to meet him at the bottom of the stairs.

"That was very good!" She praised. He rolled his eyes, walking a flight of stairs should not be a praiseworthy ordeal, although truth be told he was quite pleased he had done it under his own power, considering three days ago he was not able to get up at all.

Now that he was on flat ground, the going was a bit easier. He had no idea how much upper body muscle was used when going up or down a flight of stairs. He was able to use his right arm again, although it was still quite painful.

Reginald had waxed poetic last night about the sight of his muscle tissue, stating he had only ever got to examine those muscles in cadavers before, and they were an entirely different hue when inside a living being. David was certain he meant that to be a compliment somehow and had given Reginald a dry, "Yes, I'm glad my stabbing served the good of edifying your education."

He had spent a few hours at his mother's bedside earlier that morning. They had spent a little time going over the estate business, but mainly they had just talked.

Now that he knew that he was Annabelle and George's son, he had any number of questions about his birth parents. The Duchess had indulged him and told him a few stories about Annabelle, how she had fallen in love at first sight with George, the first time that Dorian had come to call on her. Dorian had arrived in his newly painted carriage, and George had been in full gold and red livery. Annabelle was supposed to ride in the carriage with Drusilla to serve as chaperon, but after one look at George insisted she got motion sickness inside carriages and asked to ride up top, next to George. Drusilla and Dorian were thrilled for some alone time. Annabelle proved to be the worst chaperon in history over the course of the next several weeks. Dorian proposed to Drusilla, and not a week later, George asked Annabelle to be his wife.

"You're built like George, and you have his brown eyes, and Annabelle's curly dark locks. George's hair was a bit lighter than hers, a dark sandy color, I'd say." She'd told him.

He had his father's eyes. It had been a point of curiosity his entire life, knowing his mother had green eyes and that the Duke, Dorian had blue eyes.

He and Clarissa made their way through the portico towards the garden beyond. The roses seemed to be in full bloom now. He turned to Clarissa,

"We could have our wedding ceremony out here, you would get the chance to wear Mother's dress that you told me about," he offered.

"I'd like that. Maybe in a few days hence, after they catch Lord Grey, and we put this all behind us."

"I will be glad when this is all over. Then we can spend the Duchess's last days in peace."

"I spent some time with her this morning. I have to admit that knowing she is not my real mother, actually makes me like her more. Is that strange?"

"No...I think I have the opposite reaction. I always thought of Annabelle as my mother, and knowing that the Duchess was the one who birthed me, made me feel a bit more distant from her."

"Do you forgive our mothers for what they

did?"

"Forgive is a difficult word. I understand that they were in a situation, and believe that what they did was best for everyone. We were but babes weren't we? They did not know us, did not know the people that we would become."

"It saddens me; I never knew that Annabelle was my mother. I loved her, of course, but did not have that feeling of kinship with her. I am sorry for that."

"She was a good mother. I see much of her in you, the dimple in your cheek when you smile, the color and texture of your hair. Your deep capacity for love," Clarissa told him, taking his left hand in hers as they walked.

"How did I never see it? How did I not know, or sense the truth, until now? That's what I don't understand." David asked, shaking his head at his own ignorance.

Clarissa shrugged "We believe the truth that is given to us. We were ignorant of the facts. Now we know. Does it really make any difference? We can't change the past. In truth, I know I would never want to. If I had been raised as the daughter of the Duke and Duchess and you had been raised as the son of the footman and the ladies' maid do you believe we would we be married now?" Clarissa pondered.

"I don't know. I cannot imagine any scenario where my love for you would not have been the same, though I fear I would not have found you as approachable."

"Then it is a good thing, what happened, isn't it? I refuse to regret it," Clarissa declared.

They had strolled among the roses to the low brick wall that lined the property along it's south side. They could clearly see the long and winding drive that lead from the road to the house.

They were cresting a rise in the landscape when they both saw it, a group of seven men on horseback coming down the road. All with hats pulled down low and kerchiefs covering their faces, even from this distance it was evident that they all were armed with pistols and rifles. David tensed, and grabbed Clarissa and they both crouched below the edge of the stone wall. The sound of the horse's hooves grew closer and it became obvious that they had not continued down the road, but turned toward the house and here now heading up the drive.

"Who are they?" Clarissa whispered anxiously.

"I was hoping you'd tell me," David replied. "You don't recognize any of them?"

"No, they look a bit…rough."

"They do. They'll be coming up to the gate, once they pass it, they'll certainly see us," David surmised.

"What should we do?

"They are being quite bold, coming up to the house in the middle of the day. I can't imagine they mean us well."

They were perhaps a hundred yards to the stable, which was the nearest shelter. David grabbed Clarissa by the hand. "We've got to run, now!" They took off at a sprint, towards the stable, both keeping as low as possible, trying not to draw attention to themselves. Unless the men were looking in their specific direction, they might make it without being seen.

David tried to block out the burning pain in his shoulder as he ran, focusing instead on getting Clarissa to safety. As they reached the stable, they saw MacPherson, and one of the stable hands in the corral, working with a young mare.

"Mac, we saw a bunch of men with guns, heading this way!" Clarissa called out. "We need to alert everyone in the house."

MacPherson sprang into action. He sprinted into the stable and pulled a rifle off of the wall. "Go to the house, and tell Betty to get everyone into the cold cellar under the kitchen, and lock the door from the inside Including Robbie. We'll let them know when they can come out," he directed to the stable boy.

The boy took off towards the house and David went to the first horse he could see, which was Osiris, the one he had learned to ride on as a boy.

He had to get Clarissa out; he put a bridle on the horse and was reaching for the saddle when we heard a click from a few feet away. He turned to see a man, who looked somewhat familiar. Then he remembered. He'd seen him at the back of the Inn, the night of the carriage attack.

Clarissa crept over to him and placed her shaking hand in his. MacPherson was doing his best to stand in front of both of them, blocking them with his body. The man scanned first David's face, then Clarissa's, and a look of shocked fury came into his eyes.

"It seems you've been keeping things from me Mac. I can see why the Duchess was now so insistent that I keep away from you. You aren't my nephew at all, are you?"

"I don't know what you're talking about." David lied. Lord Grey pointed his gun at Clarissa, and David lunged forward, and Lord Grey redirected the gun in his direction. David stilled, but got Clarissa behind him.

"Don't you? Well it seems the Duchess was more clever than I gave her credit for. I knew her well, in her youth, you see, and this girl can be none other than her daughter, I'm sure. I've not seen that shade of gold hair since my nephew Dorian breathed his last, and those blue eyes are his, I'm sure."

He turned the gun now on MacPherson. "You knew, all along, didn't you? You've been duping me for twenty-five years. Taking my coin and misleading me, time and again. I should have done away with you years ago," he sneered.

"My Lord, I...don't know what you mean," MacPherson feigned.

"You knew the Duchess never had a son! This man is not my great nephew, at all. Which means, this estate, all of it should have been mine! You did this to me!" Lord Grey's voice rose and rose in anger.

Grey pulled the trigger, and MacPherson jerked as the bullet slammed into his chest. Clarissa screamed and David tried to grab MacPherson, before he hit the ground. MacPherson still had his own rifle in his hands which, in his last moments he pushed into David's. "Betty...Robbie..." He said, trying to convey his last desperate thoughts, looking into David's eyes.

"I'll take care of them, Mac, I swear," David promised. MacPherson nodded once and then slumped to the ground, as the last of his life blood pumped out of him. David could scarcely believe what was happening. Clarissa was still behind him and that realization shocked him into action. He took MacPherson's rifle in his hand and pointed it and as Lord Grey advanced on him he shut his eyes as he pulled the trigger. All he heard was a click.

Horrified, he opened his eyes to see a glare of pure evil directed at him from Lord Grey. "Back up!" He ordered. Just then several men came around the house, towards the stable. Without thought he flipped the gun, to hold it by the steel muzzle and swung it as hard as he could, smashing the rifle butt against Lord Grey's arm, which gave a satisfying crunch. The man stumbled back, landing on his back in the dirt, clutching his arm, cursing the air blue.

David grabbed Clarissa by the hand, and they made their escape.

They ran past the garden and towards the woods. There was a time he and Clarissa knew every inch of these woods. He hoped that knowledge was still with them.

He was vaguely aware that Lord Grey, along with the clan of men was not far behind him. Finally, he saw it, their oak tree. He pushed Clarissa up the ladder and was only one rung behind her; the men were still scrabbling about the brush, and complaining loudly. He just had time to throw himself onto the floor of the tree house and pull the ladder up behind him, when the lot of them finally burst into the clearing under the canopy of green.

He looked towards Clarissa; she was crouched low on the platform. She, like him, was trying to control her heaving breath and not make a sound. He clenched his teeth as the pain on his back seemed to ricochet throughout his shoulder and arm, making him break out in a sweat.

The men were just under the tree now, if they looked straight up, they'd see a bit of the platform base. He prayed no one looked straight up.

They had to cause a distraction, something to let them have a chance to get away.

David held Clarissa back from the edge of the platform. The tree house was more than a dozen years old, and creaking and not completely stable. David knew one of the floor boards needed replacing and was worried that it was the one underneath Clarissa's feet. He could just imagine the thing crumpling underneath their combined weight, sending them plummeting to the ground.

Chapter Thirty-Two

They could hear the men talking. She glanced towards David. He held a finger to his lips, and she knew that she best not make a sound, to draw attention to themselves, above their assailants. She nodded, wishing she did not feel quite so defenseless. She knew David was still recovering from the wound in his nodded back and not able to move with his usual nimble grace, and might not be able to defend them if Lord Grey and his minions might chance a look up. The platform was well hidden among the foliage and not visible unless one was looking straight up at the base of the tree trunk, David having pulled up the rope ladder behind them. She peered around his shoulder and could just make out a dirty urchin of a man stalking back and forth not fifteen feet below them, cursing words that Clarissa had never ever heard uttered in conversation, polite or otherwise.

David touched her hand and pointed towards a nest of acorns. He tilted his chin towards them, and then cast his eyes out towards the south. She glanced up and saw an opening in the branches and knew exactly what he meant her to do. Seems her years of casting stones on the pond might come in handy. She bent carefully and picked up several of acorns and carefully palmed one, not much heft to it, but it would do. She straightened to full height, cautious not to make a sound as she stood. She leaned back then pitched the acorn through the clearing in the branches. She heard it land in the brush a few dozen yards away, she cast a second one, a bit further, and the man called to the other men, and Lord Grey. "This way," he said, charging through the underbrush. She kept hurling acorns until she could no longer hear their footsteps.

David quickly lowered the rope ladder and preceded her down, barely containing a grunt of pain every time his weight bore down on his right side. She hitched her skirt up and tied a knot in the side to keep it out of her way before climbing down after him. As soon as her feet touched the ground David grabbed her by the hand and they took off towards the house. Hopefully they could get back to the estate before the men realized they'd been duped. As they neared the house, David veered to the left towards the stables. No one was there, with the exception of MacPherson's body. Clarissa's felt tears come to her eyes, and felt sickened seeing her old friend lifeless, lying in the straw, his blood a pool around him. David did not give her time to pause but dragged her to Osiris. Of course, the horse was not saddled, but it did have its bridle. Osiris was pawing the ground in his stall in obvious agitation.

"You can still ride bareback?" David asked, his breath heaving.

"Yes, of course," she told him. She and David had ridden Osiris bareback any number of times and she knew the horse was a steady and reliable mount, despite the grey that now dappled its once solid chestnut hide.

"I'm boosting you up." He said to Clarissa, and gave her a leg up to mount the horse. He quickly brought the reins up over the horse's head and handed them to Clarissa. "Get to the Welches, as fast as you can, and get help." He ordered.

"Aren't you coming with me?" She asked frantically.

"I can't...my mother. She's still in the house. They'll kill her. I need to save her."

"David, I can't leave you!" She tried to slide off the horse, but he held her firm, refusing to let her.

"You have to. Clary, go now! Get help. If I go with you, Grey will take his vengeance out on her, you know he will. I have to stop him," he pleaded.

"I...I will be back with Darius and Lucas. Please, just get to her, and hide, until we are back."

"No, when you get there, stay there! Send them, but lock yourself inside. We will seek you out when this is all finished. Do not come back here, do you hear me," he demanded.

She wanted to argue with him but she knew time was of the essence, it was better to just agree and deal with the ramifications later when she did come back with the Welch brothers in tow. There was no way she was leaving him to deal with these men on his own. She nodded, and he opened the door to the stall and led Osiris out and smacked the beast on the rump and Clarissa took off at a gallop across the field that divided the estate land and the Welches farm.

David turned and ran towards the house. He was shocked to see one of the footmen, William, at the base of the back steps leading towards the kitchen face down in the dirt, a pool of blood beneath his head. He took a moment to touch the man's neck, no pulse. He cursed; wishing he had a gun was in his hand. Then he remembered he knew that there were guns back in the stable where the carriage was stored. He quickly jogged back until he came to the stored carriage. He threw open the door and found the two pistols under the seat, as well as the knife. Luckily, they had been cleaned and reloaded since the last time the carriage had gone out. He slid the knife in his boot and one of the pistols tucked beneath his belt at his back. He cocked the other one and carried it close to his chest. His shoulder throbbed and his whole arm ached with all the exertion he had put it through in the last few hours. He gritted his teeth and went into the house.

He saw no trace of any of the servants, and prayed they had found safety in the cold cellar, and not all met the same demise as the footman, he had come across. He quickly went to the stairs and made his way to his mother's room. Every step he took seemed to deplete his energy a bit more, by the time he staggered into her bedroom he could feel his energy ebbing away, and felt a trickle down his back, and suspected he had opened his wound and was bleeding again.

"David, what's happened? I heard gunshots outside and shouting but that was nearly an hour ago. I was so frightened..." she cried, her voice feeble and afraid.

"Lord Grey showed up with some ruffians. I'm afraid they mean to do us all harm, Mother. I sent Clarissa to the Welches farm, to get help. I need to hide you." He realized he could not carry his mother and hold the pistol at the same time, so he carefully handed it to her. "Hold this," he ordered then picked her up in his arms. Even as light as she was, he had used up all of his reserve of strength and staggered under her weight, and tried not to think about the now steady trickle of blood running down his back. He staggered a few steps, not sure where to go, then went to the wardrobe in the corner and elbowed the door open. He climbed in and sat on the floor, with his mother in his lap and pulled the door shut behind them, leaving it open just the barest crack so he could see into the room. He could feel himself losing consciousness and prayed that the Welches would show up before Lord Grey and his horde of thugs made their way back to the house.

"This is the greatest of ironies," his mother whispered. "Twenty-five years ago, your mother went into hiding with my daughter in this very closet. She was so brave, my dear Annabelle, risking her life for a babe not of her own blood. I have no doubt she would have fought to the death for Clarissa, and I hope she knew I would fight to the death for you, too."

"I'm sure she knew," he murmured back. He felt the darkness encroaching, much like when he'd been astride the horse after being shot, but this time he did not have Lucas Welch there to whip him across the face, to keep him from sliding into the darkness. He struggled to keep his eyes open. Talk, he thought. That would keep the darkness at bay.

"Mother...why did you really try to keep Clarissa and me apart? I know what you told me then was that she would never be accepted as my Duchess, being born of the working class, but you knew...you knew she was highborn. Was it that you did not think I was good enough for her?"

"I am the first to admit that I handled that situation poorly. You have to understand, in my heart you have always been my son, but she is also my daughter, and I think of you both as my children. To see you together like that, well, it was horrifying at the time. Neither of you had really ever seen anything of the world, certainly, Clarissa had not. Sixteen is a dangerous age; you were still so young and had so much ahead of you, both. I had hoped to give Clarissa a season; pretend she was my orphaned cousin and give her, her choice of gentry to marry. I did offer her that, after you left and she turned me down flat. If she couldn't have you, she did not want anyone. I think it was then I realized I had made a terrible mistake. I tried to make amends with you, and with her. But you seemed determined to cast me in the light of oppressor, and blame me for breaking your heart. Every time you came home I was determined to make it right, and yet somehow we would end up quarreling, you and I. And Clarissa, each time you would leave she would draw into herself a little bit more, and it would be days before she would even speak to me. After a while, it was just easier not to demand you come home. When I realized I had not much time left, I sent Clarissa to you...hoping you two would find your way back to each other again."

"You wanted this? You wanted us to marry."

"I want you both to be happy, and if that is in each other's arms, I cannot argue with that."

"I thought you would always be opposed to our loving each other."

"I, more than anyone, know what it is like to love deeply, and passionately. I loved my Dorian, even though by all accounts he was a rake and a gambler, with no head for business whatsoever. But when I was with him, I felt alive in a way I have never felt since. I had two years with him. Two years of unconditional love and it was not nearly enough, but I would not trade those two years for all the gold in the world. I see that same kind of love between you and our Clarissa, and you have no idea how much joy that gives me," she told him sincerely.

"Thank you Mother, for telling me that."

"I should have told you sooner. About everything, then you would have been better prepared for this mess we are in now," she said regretfully.

"I'm not sure I would have been ready, before now. I suppose you were right in saying that I had much growing up to do. I don't think I would have been ready to marry Clary at sixteen, as much as I loved her. Now, I am ready to be the husband she deserves, and I am ready to take over the responsibility for the duchy as well. It is Clarissa's to inherit and I will do everything in my power to safeguard her legacy, if not my own."

"Not at the expense of your own life, my dear.

Please, I'd rather see Grey take it all than see you perish. I could not bear it and I'm sure Clarissa couldn't as well."

"Lord Grey is not giving up...I saw him earlier, he is so feral and cold. I would hand it over to him but I think it is too late. He means for all of us to die. I can't let that happen." As he said this, they heard a noise, the sound of several heavy steps coming down the hallway towards the bedroom. David stared intently at the crack of light between the wardrobe doors. He reached into his boot and pulled out his knife, and prayed he wouldn't have to use it. His mother still held one of his pistols and he thought best to leave it with her, in case she should need it, he still had the other one tucked into his belt at the small of his back, although, cramped as he was he wasn't in a position to reach for it. He hoped if he had to, he could reach it quickly.

The door to the bedroom opened and three men came in, all brandishing guns. Lord Grey followed behind them. "She has to be here! Search for her!" He demanded. Two of the men left the room, one remained behind and starting searching behind the curtains and under the bed. Lord Grey himself came over to the wardrobe and pulled open the doors. David's heart nearly hammered out of his chest as light flooded the wardrobe and he and his mother were discovered. He held the knife in his hand ready to jab it into Lord

Grey if he got near either of them. With his other hand, he tried to grab the pistol at his back, but the wrench of pain in his shoulder staggered him.

"Well, well…Drusilla, we meet again, and my nephew, grown. Pity, our reunion will be short lived." He said, raising his pistol, pointing it straight at them.

Chapter Thirty-Three

Clarissa gave the reins a firm shake and clutched her thighs hard against the horse, trying to get just a bit more speed out of him. She cursed that David had put her astride Osiris, the oldest-and sadly, slowest, horse in the stable. She had learned to ride astride this horse, as had David, and had great affection for the animal, but at the moment she wished she had taken Pegasus instead, the young stallion with the wild streak that had three times the speed. It seemed Osiris did seem to understand her plight as he picked up speed just as they were cresting over the hill in sight of the Welches farm. "Lucas!" she cried out "Darius! Help!" she screamed as she neared their home. She gasped in relief when she saw them both come out the farmhouse door. Thank God they were home.

"Miss Clarissa...Your Grace, what is it?" Darius demanded.

"Lord Grey, He showed up with several men, they all have guns. I think they mean to kill

David and the Duchess. Please, come, quickly," she begged.

"I'll saddle the horses, you get the guns," Lucas directed his brother, who nodded, and limped quickly back into the house. She followed Lucas to his stable but did not dismount. She let the overheated horse drink, while Lucas made quick work of saddling their mounts while she relayed the details of Lord Grey's arrival and the scuffle that broke out and her and David's escape into the woods. Darius showed up then, handed a military issue gun belt, complete with a revolver to his brother, his own, already about his waist. He then handed up a rifle, one unlike any that Clarissa had ever seen. Lucas caught her eyeing the weapon.

"Miss Clarissa, you should stay here. I am sure that is what His Grace would want." Lucas told her. If she weren't still astride her horse, she would have stomped her foot.

"No...That is my husband, and our Mother in danger! I need to go. I must. I will not get in the way, but I must go back."

"If you will not stay, Your Grace, you should go to Dr. Bishop's; Percival Darwin is still staying there. We will need his help. Then round up every able bodied man you can find and send them up to Hollister." Darius ordered. She wanted to insist she go back with them, but could see that Darius was right; this would be the more useful course of action. She nodded and took off towards Dr. Bishops, and out of the corner of her eye, saw both Darius and Lucas mount their horses and take off up the hill towards Hollister. The mile between the Welches farm and the edge of the village where Dr. Bishops home resided, seemed like an endless journey. She could tell Osiris's energy was flagging and could feel his mighty body heaving under her. Still, she pressed on. She shouted for help as soon as she was within hailing distance of the house, and both Reginald and Percival came out. She quickly told them what was going on, and they too, grabbed their guns and went for their horses. She then went through the village, shouting for help. Every door opened to her, even the vicar, and every man she saw, immediately armed up. The blacksmith had a wagon already hitched up and most of the men convened at the wagon, rather than waste time saddling up their own mounts. She was so grateful; as she watched at least a dozen men, villagers and farmers all, jump on the wagon as it made its way towards Hollister.

She followed, though her pace was considerably slower. Poor Osiris, she thought. He was doing his best. They were still half a mile from Hollister when it was obvious the animal could go no further. She slid off his back, dropping his reins to the ground, and she started to run. She ran until her lungs burned and her heartfelt near to bursting from her chest.

She heard a gunshot, from inside the house and did not even think, ignoring the shouts of Lucas and Darius to stop, she continued running straight inside and up the stairs.

Two men were at the top of the stairs and they went for her, without thinking she bent down and grabbed one of them by the arm as he reached for her and threw him over her shoulder, which unfortunately meant that he went over the edge of the stair railing and landed with a chilling thud on the floor below. The other man seeing this took off down the stairs.

She reached the Duchess's bedroom as a second shot rang out, and skid to a halt. Lord Grey wavered for a moment on his feet, blocking her view of David and Drusilla, and then as if in slow motion he slid to the floor, his gun, landing with a thump beside him. Then she saw them and her heart leapt into her throat. The Duchess was cradled in David's arms, as blood ran from her shoulder and puddled on the floor. Her hand still clenched around a pistol. A few feet before her, a gasping Lord Grey lay, his hands clutched to his throat, trying to staunch the flow of blood there. David had his hand over the wound in his mother's shoulder, although he looked none to steady. It was then she noticed the blood going down the back of his own shirt.

"Were you shot?" she asked, falling to her

knees next to him and the Duchess. She ripped up a piece of her skirt and replaced it over the wound on the Duchess's chest, forcing David to relinquish his hold.

"No...he shot her, he had the gun pointed at my head, and was going to shoot me, but she jumped up and the bullet hit her instead, then she...she shot him." David slumped over to his side, his hand clutching his mothers. "Mother... please, hold on," he begged. Clarissa concentrated on keeping pressure on the wound but she knew the Duchess, her mothers, life was ebbing away. She tried to control the sob.

"Mother, please," she pleaded, and saw the Duchess open her eyes and give them a small smile.

"My beautiful children...I love you, so. Be happy," she said and then she was gone. Clarissa felt as the last breath left her body and her heart stopped beating.

"No, no, no!" she cried "Mother...Mama, no, don't leave us!" She frantically tried to shake the Duchess, anything to bring her back.

"She's gone, Clary. We have to let her go," David said. She turned to him, where he lay on the floor, and could see the growing puddle of blood at his own back, and was struck with the fear that she was about to lose him, too.

"Reggie!" She screamed. "Come quick!" She relinquished her hold on the Duchess and went to her husband and rolled him, unresisting, over to his stomach.

She ripped the back of his shirt from the tail to the neck and pushed it aside. All of his stitches had broken, and he was still bleeding profusely. She wadded up a section of his torn shirt and pushed down hard on the wound. That is where Reginald and Percival found her, astride her husband's back, bearing down with all her might on the wound that refused to stop flowing. The room reeked with the copper scent of blood, as well as gunpowder. The Duchess lay dead beside her, and Lord Grey, gurgling, breathing his last as the blood ebbed out his body. She did not give him a spare thought, as all her attention was on David. She could not, would not let him die now.

"Let me take over." Reginald insisted and Percival pulled her aside. Reggie quickly went to work assessing the wound. "I need my bag. Percival take Clarissa out of here and get my bag from my horse." He directed.

Percival dragged Clarissa, unceremoniously, out of the room, although she fought him every step of the way. She wasn't leaving David, never again.

He handed her off to Darius and Lucas. She tried to go back in the room, but Darius caught her around the waist and held her aloft even as she kicked and tried to fight him, finally he gave her a shake and told her quite sternly she needed to stay out of the way so the doctor could do his job, to see her husband.

She took a calming breath and nodded, and finally Darius let her go. Looking down at herself, she realized she was covered in blood, the Duchess's and David's. She felt faint, and staggered, and this time Lucas was the one who caught her up in his arms.

The two men took her down the hall, until they found the room she now shared with David. They set her down on the edge of the bed, and Darius sat beside her, while Lucas went about getting a pitcher of water and some towels and pulled a clean day dress from the wardrobe.

She felt coldness come over her, and began shaking. The Duchess was dead, her mother, was dead. And David...there was so much blood. Was he dying too, at this very moment? God, she was so cold.

"I think she's going into shock." She heard Lucas voice, as if it was from a great distance. She didn't even think to struggle as together the two brothers took off her bloodied gown, and gently washed the blood from her hands, as well as her face. They pulled a clean gown over her head and buttoned her up, and then pulled the duvet from the bed and wrapped it around her. She needed to get back to David, if only she could stop shaking. She was hardly aware of Darius cradling her in his arms, and Lucas as he found a bottle of whiskey and held a tumbler to her lips, and forced her to drink. It was the first burst of heat that burned her throat that seemed to pull her out of the stupor she was in with a coughing shudder.

"There you are…come back to us Miss Clarissa. Another good sip, there." He held the glass to her lips and forced her to take another drink. This one went down a bit smoother and she started to feel the warmth pulse through her, and the shaking finally stopped, as awareness fully return.

"David…I need to go to him," she said, struggling now, to get up, but Darius held her firm.

"The doctor is still working on him. We'd just be getting in the way. He'll let us know when we can see him," Darius reassured her. "His Grace is a strong man, and he has you to live for. He'll pull through, I'm sure." He held the whiskey to her lips and she drunk again, and again until the glass was empty. She suddenly felt incredibly weary, and she could hardly keep her eyes open.

"My mother is dead," she said out loud.

"Yes, I'm sorry. The Duchess is gone," Darius said.

"Lord Grey…he is dead, too."

"Yes, it appears so."

"It's over."

"We believe so…"

"I left Osiris in the pasture," she said, "Will you have someone bring him to the stable? Give him some extra oats and apples." She felt very weary, and the whiskey made her feel warm and drowsy.

"We'll take care of everything, Your Grace," was the last thing she remembered as she drifted off.

Chapter Thirty-Four

The following days were a blur. After Dr. Bishop restitched the wound on David's back, he dealt with the bodies. MacPherson was dead, as well as William the footman. According to the rest of the servants, William had carried Robbie to the cold cellar and had left again to retrieve the Duchess, but apparently had been killed before he could complete that task. David wrote a letter commending Williams's bravery to the young man's parents, and gifted them a thousand pounds.

Two of the henchmen that Lord Grey had hired, had also perished, Lord Grey, and the Duchess, both dead of gunshot wounds.

A funeral was held for the Duchess. David saw no reason to have any sort of ceremony for the man that killed her. With Dr. Bishop's assistance, Lord Grey's body was donated to science. David sincerely hoped he did more good in death than he did in life.

MacPherson was also buried, and David honored his agreement with the man, and let Robbie go, dropping all charges against the boy. Robbie had decided to leave Hollister House. He was on the first ship to America. He had asked his mother Betty to come with him, but she refused. She'd never been more than ten miles from this village where she had grown up, and was more than content to stay there. She resigned from her post as a maid at Hollister House, although both David and Clarissa told her it was unnecessary. She decided to live with her sister in the village, and accepted a job as a housekeeper, and sometimes nurse to Dr. Bishop.

Clarissa woke up in David's arms, two months after the death of their mother. "Happy Birthday, Clary," David said, kissing her gently. She smiled with sleepy eyes at him,

"Happy Birthday, Davey." She said, snuggling closer to him. He wrapped his arms tight around her.

"I've made a decision." He told her. "I'm writing to the Queen and rescinding my title. I'm going to tell her the truth."

"Yes, perhaps it's best," Clarissa agreed.

"You aren't against this? We could very well lose everything. Be cast out with nothing," he argued. She shrugged.

"We have each other. We aren't destitute either. The Duchess left me a considerable sum in her will, enough that we could reestablish ourselves somewhere else, if we should need to. I will miss this place, of course. I've always loved Hollister House. But, not as much as I love you." Her words left David humbled.

That day he sat down and wrote a long letter to the queen, only changing a few of the details in order to protect those who had always known the secret of his identity. He explained that on his mother's deathbed, she had confessed that Duchess Drusilla and her maid Annabelle had switched babies, on their day of birth. He was in fact, not the heir, that his wife, Clarissa was the true child of the Duke and Duchess of Hollister. He also explained that with the death of Lord Grey, to his knowledge there was no male heir to inherit the title, so it was renounced, and left in the hands of the throne. He sent off the letter, with the wax seal of the Duke of Hollister, certain that it was the last time he would ever use that seal.

A week later a gold carriage arrived, with the royal crest on its door. Along with it was a missive from Queen Victoria, demanding an audience with both him and Clarissa. They packed a trunk, both wondering if this was the last they would see of Hollister House, but resigned to their fate, either way.

They arrived late the following evening at Buckingham Palace, and told they would have an audience with the Queen the next morning. The elaborate bedchamber they were shown to had a beautiful four poster bed, the largest bed that Clarissa had ever seen. After declining the need for valet or ladies' maid to assist them, they were finally left alone. David wasted no time in divesting both of them of their garments. He picked up Clarissa and threw her, naked and laughing, onto the middle of the bed and then dived onto the bed after her. His stitches had been removed the day before they left Hollister and Dr. Bishop had assured him that he could resume all of his marital duties without restriction. He fully intended to take advantage of that fact.

Starting at her toes, he kissed his way lovingly up each leg, loving how she giggled as he licked her behind the knee and sighed as he kissed his way up the inside of her thighs and how her breath stuttered and moaned as he found the center of her with his tongue, and settled there, tasting and licking and nibbling until she quaked and cried out. Only then did he take her, plunging into hot depths, knowing that no matter what the future held, this, where he was right now, within her, this was his home, where he belonged, and he knew that it was more than enough. It was everything.

He flipped over on his back, with her astride him. For a moment she was startled, but soon found the advantage of the position. He reached up and cupped her breasts, thrumming his thumbs across her nipples making her gasp. She circled her hips and rocked against him, taking him deeper, and deeper still within her, grinding herself against him, faster and faster. She was glorious, he thought. Her long blonde hair fell about them like a curtain and her eyes were glazed with desire and love for him. At the moment ecstasy took them both he looked into her eyes and was awed by the sheer beauty of finding the other half of his soul in her, in this moment, even as he was shattering, he was completely whole.

It was nearly noon the next day, when they were brought in to see the Queen. He had met her before, a few years earlier, at her coronation. He, as well as every other Duke had been presented to her, and he had solemnly given his sovereign vow to her then, as was expected. He forgot how young she was. She had married nearly seven months earlier, and was already round with child. Still, she held herself with great dignity as she sat on her throne. He bowed before her, and Clarissa executed a perfect royal curtsy.

"I received your letter, and have given it careful thought. I understand that your mothers switched you the day you were born, and kept this knowledge a secret from you. That you, Clarissa Thoroughgood, are the true child of the Duke and Duchess of Hollister." Clarissa looked towards David briefly, before directing her answer to the Queen.

"Yes, your Majesty, that is correct."

"I also understand that you, David Thoroughgood, were educated and prepared your entire life to assume the duties of the Duke."

"Yes, your Majesty, that is correct," he assured her.

"We have searched your lineage, and you were correct in your letter, there are no male heirs."

"Yes, Your Majesty," he agreed.

"It is my considered opinion that no good can come of renouncing the title of Duke of Hollister from you. There was no male heir available to fill my seat either, and it did not suffer for it, as I'm sure you would agree. I will bestow on you, David George Thoroughgood, the title of 8th Duke of Hollister, and on you Clarissa Thoroughgood, the title of Duchess of Hollister. I am assuming that you are making efforts to conceive the 9th Duke of Hollister?" She said a smile on her face. Clarissa blushed, but David only grinned.

"We are, Your Majesty."

"Actually...we have already conceived." Clarissa stated. David turned to her in stunned amazement.

"We have?" He asked. She nodded and he picked her up and spun her around, as she clung laughing to his neck. After a few moments, they both seemed to realize at once that they were still in audience to the Queen, and resumed standing at attention. The Queen seemed to think it all quite humorous.

"Well done. I trust you will both do your best to continue the line?"

"You can be assured, Your Majesty."

"Then henceforth you shall be known as the Duke and Duchess of Hollister, long may you reign." She said dismissing them. As soon as they were away from the Queen's chamber, David stopped, and pulled his wife into his arms, and kissed her tenderly.

"Are you happy?" He asked.

"Ecstatically so…I just wish the Duchess were here. I think she would have quite liked being a grandmother."

"If it is a girl, we shall call her Drusilla."

"Drusilla Annabelle, for both our mothers. If it is a boy?"

"George Dorian, for both of our fathers."

"What about you. Is this the outcome you would have wanted? You will now officially be the Duke, until death. You once said you regretted that you were never given a choice. Are you happy that this is your path now?"

"I am. I think these last few weeks, I've embraced what it means to be the Duke, and I believe I will be rather good at the job, as long as I have you by my side."

"You'll always have me by your side," she promised.

"Then I have more than I will ever need," he vowed, and kissed her, yet again.

Sandra Schehl has always had a passion for writing, history, and romance. It took her many years to finally combine these passions and become an author of Historical Romance, creating characters that leap off the page. She was born and raised in Omaha Nebraska but now calls rural Illinois home. She is happily married to her husband Doug and "mom" to an assortment of furry creatures. She is an avid board game player, film festival follower, and coffee house connoisseur.